Baby-sitters' Summer Vacation

THE BABY-SITTERS CLUB®

SUPER SPECIAL #2

Baby-sitters' Summer Vacation

ANN M. MARTIN

SCHOLASTIC INC.

For Jean, Barry, and Bonkie

Copyright © 1989 by Ann M. Martin

This book was originally published in paperback by Scholastic Inc. in 1989.

All rights reserved. Published by Scholastic Inc., *Publishers since 1920.* SCHOLASTIC, THE BABY-SITTERS CLUB, and associated logos are trademarks and/or registered trademarks of Scholastic Inc.

The publisher does not have any control over and does not assume any responsibility for author or third-party websites or their content.

No part of this publication may be reproduced, stored in a retrieval system, or transmitted in any form or by any means, electronic, mechanical, photocopying, recording, or otherwise, without written permission of the publisher. For information regarding permission, write to Scholastic Inc., Attention: Permissions Department, 557 Broadway, New York, NY 10012.

This book is a work of fiction. Names, characters, places, and incidents are either the product of the author's imagination or are used fictitiously, and any resemblance to actual persons, living or dead, business establishments, events, or locales is entirely coincidental.

ISBN 978-1-338-81468-2

10 9 8 7 6 5 4 3 2 1   23 24 25 26 27

Printed in the U.S.A. 40
This edition first printing 2023

Book design by Maeve Norton

Dear Stacey,

This is your last chance! Won't you please, please, please come to Camp Moosehead with us this summer? You can still sign up. We know because it took Mary Anne all this time to make up her mind about camp and she just signed up last week and the director said "Oh, thank goodness, we need more CITs." (Really, she did say that.) But the deadline is coming up in two weeks.

So you've got time if you hurry. Being CITs together would be so much fun, especially since now all the rest of the Baby-sitters Club (well, except for Shannon Kilbourne) is going to be at Camp Moosehead for two weeks. Even Logan is going. Won't the New York branch of the club please come? Think of the fun we'll have—swimming, boating, hiking, meeting boy CITs.

Stacey, come on!

Love, Kristy,
Mary Anne, LOGAN, Dawn,
JESSI, and Mallory

CHAPTER 1

Saturday

Dear Mom and Dad,

Well, here I am at Camp Moosehead. I have to admit it's very pretty, which is a relief. I really thought I'd miss skyscrapers and cars and especially department stores. But I don't—yet. The ride up here was weird, since I don't know any of the kids, and they mostly knew each other. When I got off the bus, though, what a reunion! The Baby-sitters Club was together again!

Mr. and Mrs. Edward McGill

14 West 81st street, Apt. 12-E

New York, NY 10000

I'll never understand. How did this happen?

I, Stacey McGill, am a New York City girl. I love the feel of concrete under my feet. I love the sight of tall buildings. I especially love the sight of a really prime department store, such as Bloomingdale's. Grass and trees and lakes? I can take them or leave them. Or I can visit Central Park. So how did I wind up going to Camp Moosehead as a counselor-in-training for two weeks? Well, it had to do with my friends in Connecticut. I lived in Stoneybrook, Connecticut, for a year, and right after I moved there, I joined a group called the Baby-sitters Club. The girls in the club became my friends, and we stayed friends after my parents and I moved back to New York.

One day I received a letter from my friends saying that they were going to Camp Moosehead as CITs for two weeks. They said being a CIT is better than being a camper or a counselor because you get all the fun of being a camper, plus extra privileges, and all the privileges of being a counselor, plus extra fun. Then they said, wouldn't I like to be a CIT at Camp Moosehead for two weeks, too?

I wrote back and said NO! I told them all the stuff about concrete and tall buildings and Bloomingdale's and Central Park. They wrote back and said, But Stacey, it's only for two weeks.

I wrote back and said, So what? This went on for quite awhile, until finally they convinced me to go. Anyway, how could I miss out on something the rest of the club was going to do? I couldn't. So I gave in.

I decided to do something special, though. I decided that if I was going to make this supreme effort — if I was going to give up two weeks of a perfectly good summer plus Bloomingdale's and my baby-sitting jobs in New York and all the rest — then I wanted some sort of a record of my adventure in the woods. I was going to keep a notebook about the two weeks at Camp Moosehead, and make all my friends write in it, too. When it was finished, it would be my book. We would all write in it, but the book would be mine. Of course, I would let the others read it any time they wanted.

So here is Chapter One. I get to write the first chapter because the book is my idea and I'm bringing the notebook to camp with me from New York, and besides, none of the other club members knows about it yet. They will soon, though. Since the start of the Baby-sitters Club, Kristy has made the rest of us write up every single sitting job we ever went on. There's a huge fat notebook full of our experiences. Kristy could order us to do something like this because she's the club president, the boss. Now it is my turn to be the boss.

So. Here I am at Camp Moosehead.

At nine o'clock this morning, a whole flock of campers, counselors, CITs, and junior CITs gathered in front of a building on 34th Street near Park Avenue. It was the meeting spot for anyone in Manhattan going upstate to Camp Moosehead.

You should have been there. I will never forget that scene. It was a mob of parents, and of kids ages six to twenty. (Well, the twenty-year-olds were the counselors, and they weren't exactly kids.) Half the people in the crowd were crying. That half was the parents. Also a few of the youngest kids were crying. They were saying things like, "Is my teddy *really* going to be okay smushed into my suitcase for three hours?" and "What if they make me eat *tur*nips at camp?"

The parents were saying things like, "Oh, my baby. Going away for two entire weeks. You're growing up so fast. You'll probably come back taller than I am." (And hopefully smarter, I thought.)

My own personal mother was saying, "Oh, my baby. Going away for two entire weeks. You're growing up so fast. What am I going to *do* while you're gone?"

She dabbed at her eyes with a soggy Kleenex.

"You could go to Bloomingdale's," I suggested.

My father laughed. "She could move *into* Bloomingdale's."

Then we all laughed.

While the laughing and crying were going on, the counselors had been loading suitcases and sleeping bags and knapsacks into the luggage compartments under two buses parked at the curb. Since most of us would be gone for only two weeks, not the whole summer, we didn't need to pack up trunks and a ton of other stuff. Only four kids did. Anyway, it barely mattered what we packed in, because in everybody's suitcase were the same things: about three hundred pairs each of Camp Moosehead T-shirts, shorts, socks, sweaters, and nightshirts. (We were allowed to wear our own underwear and sneakers, thank goodness.) And on every article of clothing, including the socks, was a moose head.

By the time all that Camp Moosehead stuff had been stowed under the buses, the laughing and crying had pretty much stopped. Everyone was running out of things to say. But as soon as one of the counselors shouted, "Okay, all aboard!" the talking and the good-byes began again.

"Eat *all* your vegetables," one father said.

"Don't forget to feed my goldfish!" called out a little girl.

"Are you *sure* my teddy won't suffocate in the suitcase?" asked the worried-looking boy.

"Bloomingdale's won't be the same without you." That was Mom.

"Right. It'll go broke." That was Dad.

This was getting embarrassing. So I hugged my parents and joined the line of kids that was streaming onto one of the buses. As I climbed the steps, I turned around to wave at Mom and Dad.

"Good-bye! Watch what you eat!" they called. And my mother added, "Have fun and be careful!"

It never, never, never, never, ever fails. Mom says, "Have fun and be careful," each time we say good-bye in New York. She is neurotic about it.

As nervous as I was about stepping onto a bus full of strangers, I did just that. While I was doing so I wondered, on an embarrassment scale of one to ten, just how bad "Watch what you eat" and "Have fun and be careful" were. I was about to rate them an eight when I heard another parent call out, "Remember to take your vitamins!" Well, there you go. That was a definite nine. I dropped my parents' rating to a six and tried to decide where to sit. All the campers were sitting together, sharing seats, taking up entire rows. I looked for the CITs. They were doing the same thing, and I didn't see anyone sitting alone. So I started a new seat, hoping someone decent would join me.

Guess what? *No one* sat next to me. The bus wasn't full. Talk about embarrassing. I guess most of these kids had been to Camp Moosehead before, so they already knew each other. Why should they talk to someone they didn't know? It would have been nice, though. I mean, what was I supposed to do? I could pull out a book and start reading, but reading on a bus usually gives me a headache. Besides, I'd look like a total dork. (Too bad, because I was in the middle of *The Catcher in the Rye*, which is wonderful.)

So I just sat there, stared out the window, and daydreamed.

The bus cruised up Park Avenue for awhile. Then we drove over a bridge and out of the city. That is an exciting thing to do, no matter how often you do it. I watched the scenery go by. I listened to the CITs in front of me. They were talking about makeup and clothes (not Camp Moosehead clothes) and Bloomingdale's. I wanted to join their conversation, but I didn't. I'm bold, but not that bold.

I remembered the first time the girls in the Baby-sitters Club called me up to beg me to come to Camp Moosehead with them. Until then, they'd been writing letters saying, Please come, and I'd been writing back saying, No way, but the phone call made me start thinking. That night at dinner I brought the subject up with my parents. The first thing they said was, "But, Stacey, what about your diabetes?" (They say this whenever I want to do anything new.)

I replied, "What about it? I'll bring my supplies with me. I've been away for two weeks before."

My parents were not convinced.

Diabetes is a disease which affects your blood sugar level. I have to give myself something called insulin twice a day and stick to a strict diet, which means hardly any sugar or sweets. If I don't, I could get really sick.

Anyway, after quite a while, my friends convinced me to go to camp, and I convinced my parents to let me go to camp, diabetes and all. It was a tough battle, but for heaven's sake, what are they going to do when I want to go away to college? I'm already thirteen.

The bus rattled on and on . . . and on. We traveled along a highway, then a country road, then a smaller, narrower country road, and then a dirt road. Finally we drove under a fake wooden signpost that said CAMP MOOSEHEAD. A picture of that moose head was at either end of the sign. A little way ahead of us I could see other buses. Kids (well, girls) were pouring off of them. (The boys would be driven around to the other side of the lake to their side of the camp.) Suitcases were being unloaded from the buses.

One of the counselors on our bus stood up. "Okay, all girls out!" she called. There was a stampede. I was nearly trampled.

But as soon as I set foot on Camp Moosehead ground, I heard a familiar voice cry, "There she is! Hey, Stace! Stacey!"

It was Claudia Kishi, my best friend from Stoneybrook. With her were Kristy Thomas, Dawn Schafer, Jessi Ramsey, Mary Anne Spier, and Mallory Pike.

"Hi, you guys!" I was *so* glad to see them. I ran to them and we began jumping up and down. Then I tried to hug all of them at once, but it didn't work.

"Together again! The Baby-sitters Club is together again!" exclaimed Claudia.

We've been together a few times since I moved away from Connecticut, and each reunion is great.

The seven of us were laughing and talking and kidding about our dumb Camp Moosehead outfits, which look a little like gym suits, when a

11

small figure came flying toward me and threw her arms around my waist. It was Charlotte Johanssen. She's from Stoneybrook, too. She's eight and was going to be a camper at Moosehead while my friends and I were there as CITs. I was her favorite baby-sitter when I lived in Connecticut. We miss each other a lot.

"Hiya, Char!" I said.

Charlotte hugged me and hugged me. When she finally pulled away, she left wet spots on my moose head shirt and I saw that her eyes were red from crying. Crying over our reunion? Crying from excitement over arriving at camp? I was about to ask her what was going on, when a voice came over a loudspeaker.

"Attention, campers and counselors. Attention, campers and counselors. Please assemble for cabin assignments."

CHAPTER 2

Saturday

Dear Charlie, Sam, Andrew, and Emily,

Well, we got to Camp Moosehead safely. The bus ride was something else. A lot of interesting things happened. And your own brother was in on half the stuff. But somehow we reached the camp. One of the first people we saw was Stacey. What a reunion! Now we are in our cabins. We have unpacked. I've got the eight-year-olds. There's a counselor, me, another CIT, and six campers in my cabin. Guess who two of the campers are—Charlotte Johanssen and Becca Ramsey!

Love,

Your sister,

Kristy

Charlie and Sam Thomas

Andrew and Emily Brewer

1210 McLelland Road

Stoneybrook, CT 06800

Well, the tables have turned, the shoe is on the other foot, and all that stuff. Stacey is making us write a book. Even Logan is writing entries for it. I guess Stacey can make us do that. After all, I've made everyone write in the club notebook for ages now.

So here goes. . . . Well, our summer vacation all started because of Dawn. Dawn lives with her mother, and she and her mom own the movie *The Parent Trap*. They also have *Meatballs*. Both movies are about camp, and Dawn watches *The Parent Trap* at least once a week, maybe because her parents are divorced and she would like to get them together again, just like the twins in the movie do with their parents. Anyway, after the members of the Baby-sitters Club had seen *The Parent Trap* for, oh, the six hundred and fiftieth time, somebody (me, I think) said, "Wouldn't it be fun if we could go to camp? I've never been."

"Me neither," said Jessi Ramsey, Mary Anne Spier, and Mallory Pike.

"I went once when I was seven," said Claudia Kishi.

"I went for three summers in California," said Dawn. (Dawn grew up in California.)

Anyway, to make a long story very, very, very

short, we found out about Camp Moosehead and we found out that us thirteen-year-olds (me, Claudia, Dawn, Mary Anne, Logan, and Stacey) could be CITs. Jessi and Mal would probably have to be regular campers, since they're eleven. Then our parents said we could go.

So that's how today we wound up boarding a bus to Camp Moosehead, which is in New York State. Only us baby-sitters weren't the only Stoneybrookers going. Word about camp spread fast, and suddenly a lot of our younger brothers and sisters and their friends, and some of the kids our club sits for, wanted to go to Camp Moosehead as campers. So my younger brother, David Michael, and my stepsister, Karen, were going. Jessi's little sister, Becca, was going. And most of Mallory's younger brothers and sisters were going. She's got seven, and all but Claire, the very youngest (she's *too* young) boarded the Camp Moosehead bus today. So did Nancy Dawes, a friend of Karen's; Charlotte Johanssen, Becca's good friend; Buddy Barrett and Matt Braddock, friends of the Pikes; Haley Braddock, Matt's older sister; and Jackie and Shea Rodowsky, kids our club sits for. That made twenty-three of us — after Stacey *finally* agreed to go, and her parents *finally* gave her permission.

The bus ride to camp was pretty interesting. So was saying good-bye as we boarded the bus in Stoneybrook. The counselors, CITs, junior CITs, and campers gathered at the parking lot of Stoneybrook High, where my big brothers go to school. Parents, brothers, sisters, and relatives were there, too. It was a mob scene.

I was there with Mom; my stepfather, Watson; Karen and David Michael (campers); my stepbrother, Andrew; and our little sister, Emily. Sam and Charlie (my big brothers) refused to come. They said the experience was going to be one long, embarrassing good-bye scene, and they wanted to avoid it completely. They said they would rather clean the house. (If Mom and Watson and Andrew and Emily actually got home to a clean house, I would . . . I would . . . well, I'd do something weird, like eat my hat.)

"Where are you guys going?" Andrew asked Karen and David Michael and me for about the twelfth time that morning. No wonder he didn't understand. We were going someplace where we could play for two weeks.

"Couldn't you just go to the playground a lot?" Andrew wanted to know.

Watson tried to explain camp again. Maybe he should rent *The Parent Trap* for Andrew.

I looked around for Mary Anne and everyone,

and stood with them in a tight, excited bu
We talked a lot, nervously.

"I can't wait to see Stacey!" cried Claudia, but then she grew solemn. "I'm worried about leaving Mimi, though." (Claudia's grandmother is not in such great shape.)

"*I* can't wait to go boating!" said Dawn. (There's a famous boating scene in *The Parent Trap*.)

Not everyone was as excited as we were, though. Charlotte Johanssen was crying. She was standing with her parents, and tears were streaming down her face. "I don't want to go away!" she was wailing.

I was a little surprised when Charlotte had said she wanted to be one of the kids to go to overnight camp. She is shy, has stage fright, doesn't have many friends, and sticks close to home. She's smart and sweet and kind and all those good things, but she's awfully attached to her home and parents. She's also attached to her best friend, Becca Ramsey, and her former best baby-sitter, Stacey. I think she wanted to be with Becca and Stacey for two weeks. Plus, the Camp Moosehead brochure is pretty glitzy and has these nice pictures of kids going on nature walks and making lanyards in arts and crafts. Char loves stuff like that, so she got hooked on the idea of camp. But now that the moment had arrived . . .

And it really had arrived. A school bus with the words CAMP MOOSEHEAD on either side and these pictures of moose heads had just pulled into the parking lot.

"It's here! It's here!" shouted David Michael. Unlike Charlotte, my brother was so excited about going away from home that he hadn't been able to sleep for two nights. I think Mom was a little hurt.

Several counselors jumped off the bus and began loading our gear in the compartment underneath. Around me I heard different kinds of comments — and shouts and laughter and tears.

"Call us any time, honey," said Dr. Johanssen, Charlotte's mother.

Charlotte's reply was a muffled sob.

"Behave yourself," Mom told David Michael.

"Behave yourself," Watson told Karen. Since she's only six, she'd be one of the youngest campers, but she can be awfully energetic.

"Dad, what if I don't like camp?" Vanessa Pike asked her father. Vanessa is a daydreamer, a poet, who's not terribly outgoing or athletic.

"If you really don't like it, we'll come get you," he replied, "but give it a fair try first, okay? At least a week and a half."

"Oh, *Dad*," said Vanessa, and giggled.

Us kids were starting to file onto the bus. I hugged Mom hard. I kissed Watson on the cheek. I tickled Andrew and Emily. Then I took Karen by the hand (she *is* only six), and stepped onto the bus.

All the younger kids — Becca, Karen, the Braddocks, Charlotte, the others — sat together. So did us sitters. There were already a few other kids from a nearby town on the bus and *they* were sitting in a group. We kind of smiled at them. Then we began waving out the windows to our moms and dads and stepparents and grandmas. I was sitting by the window and Mary Anne was next to me. She leaned across me to wave frantically to her father and nearly fell out.

The bus pulled out of the parking lot. It drove down the street, through Stoneybrook, and onto the highway. We were on our way!

A few interesting things happened on that bus ride. The first one was that Jackie Rodowsky, our totally accident-prone walking disaster, shouted, "Camp Moosehead, here we come!" and waved his special Camp Moosehead baseball cap out the window. The wind caught it and blew it away. We all watched it bounce down the highway.

"All heads, hands, and arms *must* stay in the bus!" announced a counselor.

Not too much later, Margo Pike, Mallory's

second-to-youngest sister, got out of her seat, hurried up the aisle to Mallory, and said in a shaky voice, "I don't feel so good." Margo gets airsick, carsick, sick on amusement park rides, etc. Well, now we could add bussick to the list.

Oh, brother, I thought. What a mess this will be.

But Mallory was prepared. She pulled a garbage bag out of her pocket, opened it up (just in time), and Margo puked in that. Then people switched around so Mal and Margo could sit together in the front seat, and after that Margo was okay.

We were about halfway to Camp Moosehead when my dumb brother suddenly shouted, "Hey, you guys, let's sing 'Ninety-nine Bottles of Beer on the Wall.'" (He shouted this to the bus in general.)

David Michael is always starting this song and it drives me crazy. Only this time he started with, "*One million bottles of beer on the wall . . .*"

I laughed. "Good joke, David Michael," I said.

But nobody else thought it was a joke. When the kids finished that verse, they sang, "*Nine hundred ninety-nine thousand nine hundred ninety-nine bottles of beer on the wall, nine hundred ninety-nine thousand nine hundred ninety-nine bottles of beer, take one down . . .*"

They sang and sang and sang. By the time we reached Camp Moosehead, they were still in the nine hundred ninety-nine thousands. But I barely

cared. We were at camp! The girls on
piled off. The boys were going to be a.
around the lake to the other side of Camp
Moosehead.

The counselors were still unloading the girls'
luggage when another bus drove into the parking
lot — and Stacey got off!

"Reunion!" I shouted, and my friends and I
dashed to her.

I didn't know it, but someone was following
us — Charlotte Johanssen. She had seemed okay
on the bus, sitting with Becca, playing magnetic
checkers, and occasionally joining in on "One
Million Bottles of Beer on the Wall." But now she
was a mess.

She threw herself at Stacey, crying hard. I
think she said, "Stacey, I want to go *home*!" but it
was hard to tell because just then a voice came
over a loudspeaker.

"Attention, campers and counselors. Attention,
campers and counselors. Please assemble for
cabin assignments."

The buses headed for the boys' side of camp. I
waved good-bye to David Michael.

Camp Moosehead had officially begun.

CHAPTER 3

Satruday

Dear Mimi,

Hi, how are you? Fine, I hope. I'm at camp it is so so fun. Well we havn't done to much so far but I can tell it's going to be fun. I havn't been away for a hole day yet but I miss you all ready. I realy realy hop your ok. So far we have are cabin asinments. Guess who's in my cabin, Vanesa Pike and Haley Bradock. Tonight we have a group sing.

Love,
your Claudia

Mrs. L Yamamoto
58 Bradford Court
Stoneybrook, CT 06800

Attention, campers and counselors. Attention, campers and counselors. Please assemble for cabin assignments."

We were in the middle of our Baby-sitters Club reunion, and Charlotte Johanssen was crying all over Stacey (while I wanted to hug her), and then that voice came over the loudspeaker.

"What are cabin assignments?" asked Charlotte as she pulled away from Stacey. She wiped her sleeve across her eyes and sniffled. Mary Anne handed her a Kleenex.

"That's when everyone finds out which cabin they'll be staying in while they're here," said Dawn knowingly. "We'll probably group together now — counselors, campers, and CITs."

"And junior CITs," added Mallory.

"And junior CITs," Dawn repeated.

Mallory and Jessi had been made junior CITs. It's a long story.

"Oh, I hope I'm in Becca's cabin," said Charlotte anxiously.

That announcement practically caused a riot as everyone rushed for this big open area around a flagpole, where the head of the camp was going to organize us girls. Since it looked like the organizing might take awhile, Stacey and I hung back from the rest of our friends for a few minutes.

I threw my arms around her. "It's so good to

see you!" I exclaimed. "You look fabulous! What did you do to your hair?" I pulled away and held her at arm's length the way this one aunt of mine always does to me.

"Body wave," Stacey replied. "I swore up and down that I wouldn't perm it again, and then it grew out and looked funny — kind of lank. And orange-ish instead of blonde. So I settled on getting a body wave. In fact, Mom *told* me to get a body wave."

"Your own *mother*?" Unheard of.

Stacey nodded.

"Well, I think you did the right thing."

"Thanks. How are you? How's Mimi?"

"I'm fine. Mimi's okay," I replied. "Not great, but okay. It's funny. You know all the physical therapy she's been getting since she had the stroke?"

"Yup," said Stacey. And we hurried a little to start catching up with everyone.

"Well, it seems to be helping. We keep seeing improvement. But only in her body. Not in her mind. She's mixed up her sentences and forgotten words since the stroke, but now she's saying really weird things. Like, she'll wander into my room and ask me what dress Patsy stole for the dance."

"Huh?"

"I know. What does that mean? Who's Patsy?

What dance? And why *steal* a dress instead of buy one or borrow one? I don't get it."

We had joined the others and were standing at the edge of the big crowd of kids. Stacey started to say something to me — to answer my questions, maybe — when we realized that the camp director was reading off lists of names and we better pay attention to her.

I knew she was the camp director because her picture was in the camp brochure. In a lot of places. Her husband is the director of the boys' side of the camp, across the lake. Her name is Mrs. Means.

Mrs. Means. Funny.

And just as I was thinking that, I heard a girl next to me nudge her friend and say, "Old Meanie hasn't changed a bit."

Her friend giggled. "Yeah. Same as ever."

So *I* nudged Stacey and said, "Hey, Stace, they call Mrs. Means 'Old Meanie.'"

Stacey grinned.

We went back to listening to Old Meanie.

"In Meghan's cabin," she was saying, "the CITs are Sally Troner and Claudia Kishi. The campers are as follows." She rattled off a list of six campers, including Vanessa and Haley.

"Well," I said, "here goes. This is it." I looked at Stacey and at tearstained Charlotte. "I guess

I'll see you later this afternoon or at supper or something."

"Bye, Claud," said Stacey nervously.

I joined a group of girls that was gathering near Mrs. Means. "Hi," I said to the tallest one. "Are you Meghan?"

"Yup," the girl answered cheerfully.

"Good. Then this is the right group. I'm Claudia Kishi."

"Oh, our other CIT. Terrific. I think we're all here."

Gathered around me were Meghan, Vanessa, Haley, four other girls about Vanessa's age, and an older girl whom I guessed was Sally, my co-CIT. She wore her brown hair in a French braid and reminded me a little of Stacey — sophisticated, but probably not snobby. I hoped we would be friends.

"Well," said Meghan, "let's introduce ourselves, even though we'll probably forget everyone's names right away."

We laughed but agreed to try it. "I'm Meghan," Meghan began, "and I'm your counselor. We're in Cabin Nine-A, by the way, because you campers are nine years old, and we're one of the two nine-year-old groups. Isn't that an original way to name the cabins?"

More laughter. The introductions continued.

The other four girls turned out to be Leeann, Brandy, Jayme, and Gail. I didn't remember their last names. I hoped I wouldn't need to.

"Okay, now comes the complicated part," said Meghan.

"Trying to repeat the names?" asked Sally.

Meghan smiled. (I definitely liked both Meghan and Sally.) "Nope," said Meghan. "Getting our luggage to Cabin Nine-A."

It really was sort of a pain. First we had to find our bags, and of course everyone else was looking for theirs, too. The first time our group thought we'd gotten all our suitcases and knapsacks together, Jayme said, "Uh-oh. Where's my Garfield bag?"

We found the Garfield bag and started up a path away from the crowd and into the woods. Then Vanessa said, "Um, Claudia? I don't think this is my suitcase."

We opened it. It wasn't.

So we had to go back. All of us.

At last, at last, at last we reached our cabin. We had walked a little way through the woods, but when I turned around to look behind me, I could still see the flagpole — the center of the camp — Old Meanie and a group of girls clustered around it.

"Here we are," announced Meghan. "Home disgusting home."

Vanessa Pike burst into giggles.

I took a good look at Cabin 9-A. It was half of a bigger cabin. Guess what the other half of the bigger cabin was called? You got it — 9-B. Another group of nine-year-olds, their counselor, and their CITs would bunk in 9-B.

Our cabin looked pretty much the way you'd imagine, especially if you've seen *The Parent Trap* and *Meatballs*. It and everything in it was wooden. The outside of the cabin was made from that rough wood — logs with the bark still on. A porch stretched across the front of 9-A and 9-B. Inside 9-A were four bunk beds for the campers and CITs, and one single bed with a curtain that could be drawn around it. That was for Meghan.

Counselors get a little privacy.

Vanessa and Haley immediately claimed a bunk for themselves. Then Sally and I took a bunk. CITs ought to stick together, we thought. Jayme and Leeann seemed to have been going to Camp Moosehead together for years, so they took the third bunk, and Gail and Brandy were left with the fourth.

When the bunks had been claimed, everyone got kind of quiet — for about five seconds. Then

Meghan suggested that we unpack. There were shelves along the walls and we were supposed to put our stuff on them and stow our suitcases in the cabin's one closet.

"The room will stay neater that way," said Meghan.

So we unpacked. And we unrolled our sleeping bags on our bunks. While we did that, we began talking.

"Where do we, you know, go to the bathroom?" asked Haley, looking around the cabin suspiciously.

"The bathrooms are separate cabins," replied Jayme. "Group bathrooms."

"Ew," said Haley.

The campers started laughing.

I climbed down from my place on the top bunk to see Sally, who was below. (I stepped on her hand on the way, but she was very good-natured about it.)

"Guess what," she said, when I told her I hadn't been to Camp Moosehead before, "there's a canteen near the recreation hall where you can buy postcards and toothpaste and candy bars and things." (Junk food — yum!) "*And* us CITs get to have dances and stuff with the boy CITs."

Really?! Camp Moosehead was looking better every second!

CHAPTER 4

                                        Saturday

Dear Mama and Daddy,

    Here I am at Camp Moosehead. We got here safely
and Becca is just fine, so don't worry about her.
Charlotte is pretty homesick already, but she knows
an awful lot of people here, so I think she'll be okay.
Becca and Kristy will take care of her. (They're all
in the same cabin.) Guess what—Mallory and I are in
the same cabin, too! It's really half of a bigger cabin,
and Dawn is a CIT in the other half. Our cabin is 11-B.
Hers is 11-A.

    I miss you, I miss you, I love you, I love you.
    X X X   X X   O O O O O

                                WBS, Jessi
                        (WBS means Write Back Soon.)

Mr and Mrs. John Ramsey
612 Fawcett Avenue
Stoneybrook, CT 06800

Oh, boy. My first time at camp. I'm not really nervous. . . . No, that isn't true. I am nervous. But I'm nervous about something most of the other kids here don't even have to think about. I'm nervous because I'm one of the very few Black kids at Camp Moosehead. My sister Becca's here, of course, and I've seen two or three other Black campers. But mostly everyone is white.

I guess I should be used to that by now. I'm one of the few Black people in Stoneybrook Middle School — in Stoneybrook itself — and I'm one of the few Black dancers at my ballet school. Still, I feel uncomfortable. I always wonder if I'll fit in. Thank goodness for Mallory. Having my best friend here sure makes a difference.

Mal and I are junior CITs, by the way. We're the only junior CITs at the whole camp. We wanted to be CITs so badly that when our parents helped us fill out our camp applications, we added a whole paragraph after the place where it said "Comments." We each wrote: "I am a baby-sitter. I belong to a group called the Baby-sitters Club. We take care of children of all ages, sometimes even babies (but not too often). I have lots of experience with children. I would very, very, very, very, very much like to be a CIT. Could you please take this into consideration?"

Mrs. Means wrote back and said that she

wished she could let us be CITs, but that the rule is a CIT must be at least thirteen years old. Then she said maybe we could be junior CITs and help out with the younger campers, like in arts and crafts or on some special project.

Mal and I felt pretty special. That arrangement was good enough for us.

These are the other people in Cabin 11-B: Autumn, our counselor; Gwen and Corinne, our CITs; and Mandi, Maureen, Mary Oppenheimer, and Mary Travis, the other campers.

WAHH! Every camper except me has a name beginning with Ma-, and two of them are named Mary. I sure stick out. And I was positive I wouldn't remember anyone's name except Mallory's.

When us girls from 11-B reached our cabin, we stepped inside and immediately made mad dashes to claim our bunk beds. Well, Mal and I made a mad dash. We wanted to be sure to share a bunk. But the other campers hung back, staring at us. Then they sauntered around and chose bunks as if they couldn't care less who they shared with.

Mal and I felt like great big babies. We knew we'd done something wrong. We just weren't sure what.

When all the sauntering around was over, Corinne and Gwen, the CITs, were sharing one bunk, Mandi and Maureen were sharing another, and the two Marys took the fourth. Autumn got this private bed to herself, I guess because she's the counselor.

Autumn told us to unpack and showed us where to stow our suitcases.

Mal and I unpacked slowly. We kept asking each other where to put things (as if there were much choice. Each of us has exactly three shelves along the wall by our bunks.)

Even so, every two seconds, Mal would lean down to me from the top bed and say, "I'm putting my toothpaste and stuff on the bottom shelf on the left." Or I'd stick my head up to her and say, "I'm putting my sixteen thousand pairs of shorts along the middle shelf."

Mal giggled when I said that. A few minutes later, she leaned over again and said, "Come on up to the top bunk, Jessi."

"Why?" I asked. "I mean, the bed looks like it'll fall apart if I climb up there with you." I stood uncertainly below her.

I heard little snickers coming from Mandi, Maureen, and the Marys.

I decided the little snickers meant that the beds were safer than they looked, that I should know that, that I could easily crawl up there with Mal, and that I was stupid for thinking anything else.

So I did crawl up. And nothing happened except that the other girls stared at us.

Mallory did her best to ignore them. "I made something for us," she said.

"You did?" I replied. "What?" Mal likes to write and draw, but she doesn't often make things, so I was curious.

"Yup." Mallory reached into her almost-empty suitcase and pulled out two small bands of cloth. They were white. On each one, she'd painted a moose head and written JUNIOR CIT. "They're armbands," she told me. "We're the only junior CITs here, and I thought everyone should know it."

I wasn't so sure.

"Go on," said Mal. "Put yours on." She slid hers on and left it just below the sleeve of her Camp Moosehead T-shirt.

I hesitated. I glanced down at the M faces that were pretending to be looking at other things, but were actually watching us. I didn't want to put the armband on and be any more different from the other campers than I already was. But I did put it on — for Mal. For Mal and me.

Mal is my best friend.

As soon as I'd put the band on, though, I whispered to Mallory, "Finish putting your stuff away and then we better join the other kids. I think that would be a good idea . . . considering."

Mal took a look at the other girls, then nodded. I knew she'd understood what I'd meant. So as soon as she was done, we slid off her bunk and carried our suitcases and knapsacks to the storage closet. We had just put them away and were about to figure out some way to join the other girls, when Mrs. Means walked into our cabin.

Everyone became silent, even Autumn, who'd been talking to the counselor in 11-A. It was as if we were in school and the principal had just walked into our classroom.

"Old Meanie," I heard Mary whisper to Mary.

"They call Mrs. Means 'Old Meanie,'" I said to Mal under my breath.

Old Meanie spoke briefly to Autumn. Then she left. A sigh of relief ran through the cabin.

"Jessica and Mallory?" said Autumn.

The girls snickered again. "Ooh, you must be in trou*ble*," said Mary Travis, dragging the word out.

"Yeah, for wearing something that isn't part of the camp uniform," added Maureen.

"How could she have known about the armbands so fast?" asked Mal.

I nudged her. "They're *teasing* you."

"Oh."

Autumn stepped toward us, a smile on her face. "Junior CITs," she said. "I like that. You're the first we've had here."

"What *are* junior CITs?" asked Mandi.

Autumn tried to explain. Then she said to me, "Jessi, we've heard you're quite a dancer. Mrs. Means would like you and Mal to rehearse one of the cabins of eight-year-olds in a dance routine that they can perform in the program on Parents' Day two weeks from now. That will be your special project. It'll be a big help to us."

"Wow!" I exclaimed. "Mal, that'll be great. It'll be so much fun!"

The expression on Mal's face changed from uncertain to pleased. "You think we can really do that?" she asked. Then she added, "Of course we can. We can do anything together."

Autumn, Gwen, and Corinne wandered outside, away from us campers, which I guess gave Mary Oppenheimer the courage to say, "Yeah, you guys are the Bobbsey Twins, the way you stick together."

"The Bobbsey Twins!" cried Mandi. "They don't look like *any* kind of twins, if you know what I mean."

I sure did.

"I'll have you know that both sets of Bobbsey Twins were one boy and one girl," said Mal haughtily. "Bert and Nan, and Freddie and Flossie. How much can a boy and a girl look alike? We look more alike than they do." Mal crossed her arms and faced the other girls.

But the other girls looked pretty smug. "You still read the Bobbsey Twins books?" asked Mandi incredulously.

I stepped forward. I didn't want Mal to have to do all the defending. "Of course she does. We both do," I lied. (We've outgrown the Bobbsey Twins and are on to Nancy Drew — when we read mysteries, which isn't often. Mostly we read horse stories.)

The M girls laughed. "The Bobbsey Twins," said Mary Travis, shaking her head.

I looked helplessly at Mal. I was determined to fix this problem. I just wasn't sure how to do it.

At least we had dance rehearsals to look forward to.

CHAPTER 5

Saturday

Hi, Dad! Hi, Tigger!

How are you guys? Camp is fine. I think I have met all my bunkies and my counselor and the other CIT. I just can't believe all the things to do here. We can learn to canoe or to row a boat. And we can work on arts and crafts and take nature walks and a whole lot more.

In my cabin are a counselor, another CIT (named Randi), and six campers, including Margo Pike and Nancy Dawes (Karen Brewer's friend).

More later,
Mary Anne

Mr. Richard Spier
59 Bradford Court
Stoneybrook, CT
06800

Dad doesn't know it, but today I wrote him what was probably the least informative postcard he'd ever receive. It was certainly the least informative one I'd ever written. Suddenly I didn't know why I'd wanted to come to camp so badly. Maybe it was because it had looked like such fun in the movies — lying around on cushy beds, daydreaming about movie stars or cute boys, making neat things in arts and crafts, finding new friends to tell secrets to. But mostly what I heard about here was sports stuff. That was what the girls, even the little ones, in my cabin talked about. And the other CITs were into being totally cool. I got the idea that spending a lot of time in the arts and crafts cabin would *not* be cool.

Talk about cool, Randi, my co-CIT, reminds me so much of Claudia (only in looks) that it's weird. She has long, long dark hair, dark eyes, and extremely cool accessories. There's nothing she can do about wearing the camp outfit — she has to wear it like the rest of us — but she accessorizes it beautifully. On this first day, she wore parrot earrings (Claud has a pair of those), a braided string bracelet on one arm, a wristful of bangles on the other arm, and even an ankle bracelet over one Moosehead sock. The bracelet spells out her name. In her hair was a headband with a neon green bow attached to the side. It clashed with the green words CAMP MOOSEHEAD on her T-shirt, but who cared?

Then there are the CITs in 7-B, next door. They came over right away to meet Randi and me, and *they're* sophisticated, too. Their names are Faye and Julie. They don't look much like Stacey, but they act sort of like her (except not as nice). They're just so sophisticated and totally sure of themselves. Maybe they came up on the New York bus.

"Hi," said one as they sauntered into 7-A. "We're the CITs next door. I'm Faye, and this is Julie." Old movie-star names, I thought. Faye Dunaway, Julie Harris . . .

"Hi," replied Randi, as coolly as ever. She left her unpacking and walked over to the other girls. "I'm Randi, and this," she went on, pointing to me, "is . . . is . . . What's your name again?"

"Mary Anne," I replied, blushing. "Mary Anne Spier." I slid awkwardly off the top bed of the bunk Randi and I were sharing, and joined the other CITs.

"Have you been here before?" Julie asked me. "I don't remember seeing you."

"No. This is my first time. I've never been to camp at all."

"What'd you do? See *Meatballs* or something and think camp would be the coolest, funnest place in the world?" said Faye. She laughed loudly, as if this were how all poor, unsuspecting, new CITs found their way to Camp Moosehead.

I absolutely hate meeting new people.

I paused, pretending I'd heard Faye's joke a billion times already. I smiled at her. I even managed a little laugh. Then, "Nah," I replied. "My boyfriend's here for these two weeks. On the other side of the lake. I just wanted to be near him."

Randi, Julie, and Faye managed a three-way glance, which isn't easy. I knew exactly what they were thinking: She has a boyfriend? *She* does? She looks like a baby. (Can I help it if I'm short?) And there is *nothing* special about her. (So I hadn't thought about accessorizing at camp. I'd brought along everything on the "What to Pack" checklist. The checklist had not included parrot earrings or bangle bracelets.)

"You — you, um, have a boyfriend?" said Julie.

Faye giggled, but tried to cover it up by coughing.

"Sure," I replied. I tossed my hair over my shoulders.

"What's his name?" asked Randi.

"Logan. Logan Bruno. He's from Kentucky. He has this incredible southern accent. You should hear it."

"Faye! Faye!" one of the campers in my cabin suddenly cried. "Faye, that girl," (she pointed to Margo) "took my hairbrush."

"I did not!" Margo replied instantly. "It just looks like hers. But it's mine. If she weren't so stupid —"

"Fa-*aye*! Now she's calling me stupid!" exclaimed the girl.

"Margo," I said, "don't call her stupid. Do you know where her hairbrush is?"

"Probably in her dumb knapsack. I bet she hasn't unpacked it yet."

"Could you check your knapsack?" I asked the girl. All the while, I was wondering — how did this kid know Faye, a CIT in the other cabin? And why did she ask Faye for help instead of Randi or me or our counselor?

"My sister," Faye spoke up, "should not have to check her knapsack. If she says that girl —"

"My name is Margo Pike," Margo interrupted.

"— stole her brush, then she stole it."

"You're sisters?" I said, glancing from Faye to the other girl.

"Yes, and *my* name is Tara," said the little sister, looking pointedly at Margo.

Tara the Terror, I thought.

Margo stuck her tongue out at Tara.

Tara stuck her tongue out at Margo.

49

"I," Tara went on, not even approaching her knapsack, "bet you have never been to camp before. But *I* went to camp last year, and all my big sisters have gone to Camp Moosehead. And now Faye is a CIT and Autumn is a *counselor.*"

"Well, *my* big sister is a *junior* CIT," said Margo. "I never heard of such a thing. . . . And give me back my brush!"

By now, everyone, even Connie our counselor, was watching what was going on. I decided to show them what a good CIT I could be. I would solve the problem and stop the fight. I marched over to Tara's bunk, bent down, rifled through her knapsack, and came up with a brush that was identical to Margo's. "This yours?" I asked Tara.

"Yes," she admitted.

The other campers returned to their unpacking. The fight was over. But Margo and Nancy Dawes seemed in awe of Tara.

Tara glowered at Margo and then at me. Faye glowered at me, too.

What had gone wrong? I'd solved the hairbrush problem, hadn't I?

Connie saw us four CITs facing off, three against one. (Three against me.) "Are you guys unpacked?" she asked us.

We nodded.

"Then why don't you sit out on the porch and get to know each other?"

Obediently, we filed out the door in our cute Camp Moosehead outfits. Randi, Faye, and Julie squeezed themselves onto this big porch swing. (Wooden, of course.)

There was no room for me.

I sat on the steps. I thought of sitting with my back to them but decided not to. So I sat sideways, leaning against a post. I thought about how bold I'd been during the Tara-Margo fight. Where had that boldness come from? It was a little scary. The boldness wasn't me. And now it was fading away. My usual shyness was slipping over me like a veil.

What am I doing here? I wondered. I don't want to be sitting with these girls. They don't like me. And I'm not sure I like them. I want one of my friends — Kristy or Dawn or Claudia or Stacey or somebody.

I felt tears pricking at my eyes. But I couldn't cry. Not at the cabin. Not in front of the girls. This was neither the place nor the time to fall apart.

"So you have a boyfriend. Logan," Julie said to me.

I just nodded.

"Is he cute?"

"Mm-hmm," I could barely speak.

"*Sure* you have a boyfriend," said Faye tauntingly.

I didn't answer her.

"See?" Faye went on. "She doesn't have a boyfriend. What a fake."

If I put on some bangles and earrings, would that make a difference? Would the girls believe me then?

Through a window of the cabin I suddenly heard Tara's voice. ". . . and on Fridays, we have snake fries for dinner. You have to go out and catch your own snake. Then you fry it up and —"

"Ew, ew! I'm going to be sick!" Margo cried. "That is so gross!"

Tara laughed. She sounded satisfied.

I dashed into the cabin in case Margo really was going to be sick.

I had landed in a cabin full of hotshots, I thought. I didn't know what to do about Tara the Terror just yet. But I had an idea about how to handle the CITs. I would just have to prove to them that Logan existed.

I would show them that I was as cool as they were.

Saturday

Dear Dad and Jeff,

Well, I'm at camp again. It's been a while since I've lived in a cabin with a bunch of other girls and had to wear the same clothes day after day. (Well, not the exact same clothes, but you know what I mean.) Anyway, I think Camp Moosehead is going to be a lot of fun. The campers in my cabin are eleven years old, and they seem like a really nice group. The other CIT is nice, too, and so is our counselor. What more can I say? I'm all set for fun and adventure!

Love and Sunshine,
Dawn

The Schafers

22 Buena Vista

Palo City, CA

92800

Well, I don't know how anyone else's first day is going so far, but *mine* is great. I'm in Cabin 11-A. Eleven-year-olds, obviously. It didn't take long to figure out the creative way in which the cabins were named. These are the people in my cabin:

Charlene — our counselor. She is really, really, really nice. I hope I'm just like her when I'm eighteen. Charlene is pretty, but not in a model-ish way. Just in an outdoorsy, healthy way. You know, like those soap commercials? Also, she is understanding. She can tell when a kid is bragging and she won't believe the kid, but she won't make her feel like a liar, either. She just listens. And she is very caring. A couple of times one or another of the campers has looked a little homesick, and Charlene was right there to put an arm around her or to assure her that homesickness isn't fatal. (Charlene has a sense of humor, too.)

Amy — the other CIT. She went to Camp Moosehead last summer, but she doesn't have as much camping experience as I have. She's not exactly pretty, but she's not bad-looking, either. Her eyes are kind of close together and her nose is pointy, so she looks a little like a bird. But she's got beautiful red-blonde hair (more red than blonde) and perfect skin. I think she's very smart.

Rachel — a camper who has been going to Moosehead since she was six, the youngest you can come here. Rachel will be staying all summer. She talks very fast and tries to be friendly to everyone, which is nice, but I have a feeling she thinks her parents dump her here every summer so they can get rid of her and her brother (he's across the lake) and have time to themselves.

Shari (short for Sharilyn) — a funny camper. Actually, she's goofy, but everyone likes her a lot. I bet she's the class clown in school. Shari likes practical jokes, but I don't think she'd do anything that would hurt someone. She brought along a book of jokes and riddles and has been reading them aloud all afternoon. This is the only thing I have to say about the jokes, except that most of them are funny: If I repeated them to my mom or my grandparents, I would be grounded.

Freddie (short for I don't know what, since she won't tell us) — came up on the bus from New York City. Freddie seems a little more sophisticated than the other girls. I mean, she looks older and knows about stuff the other girls have never even heard of, such as fur storage and dining *al fresco*, which means 'outdoors.' But she gets along well with everyone, laughs at Shari's jokes, listens to Rachel even when she's talking a hundred miles an hour, etc.

Donna — has gigantic ideas and plans. I think a head doctor would describe her plans as "grandiose." Like, as soon as we reached our cabin, she said, "Hey, let's put our stuff away later, go raid the kitchen right now, and have a hot dog roast by the lake. We'll invite 11-B to join us, only they have to come in their pajamas." Donna and Shari get along great and have decided to be bunkies.

Caryn (pronounced Car-in) — has a million boyfriends, if you can believe her. She came all the way up from Princeton, New Jersey. (Her dad, who grew up around here, went to Camp Moosehead when *he* was a kid and wanted Caryn to come, too. Luckily, she loves it.) Caryn tells tall tales. We all know it, and none of us cares. She and Freddie are going to be bunkies.

Heather — Now here is the exception to the rule. The rule of our campers, that is. Heather is everything the other campers aren't, and isn't anything they are. She is very, very quiet and barely spoke two times all afternoon. In fact, I think she spoke exactly two times. When Charlene called Heather's name in roll, Heather said, "Here." And when Rachel got stuck without a bunkie and was forced to ask Heather to be hers, Heather said, "Okay."

Heather is a teeny bit on the pudgy side. She wears glasses. She parts her fine brown hair in the middle and lets it hang across her face — so that she can hide behind it, I think. (But I got a look at her face once and she's very pretty.) Heather spent all afternoon lying on her bed (the bottom bunk; Rachel claimed the top one), writing in a journal and then reading *Anne of Green Gables*. I can't tell if she's shy or frightened or stuck-up. Charlene thinks she's just quiet.

When the nine of us first arrived at Cabin 11-A, Charlene told us to unpack before we did anything else, and showed us where to put our things. That meant we had to choose bunkies right away. For Amy and me, this was no problem. CITs have to stick together, so we became bunkies.

I wondered what it would have been like if any of us club members had ended up as co-CITs, Mary Anne and I in the same cabin, for instance. I think it would have been fun, but not as broadening. "Broadening" is a word Mom has been using a lot lately. She's forever talking about the need to broaden experiences, especially her own. The only two members of the Baby-sitters Club who ended up together were Mal and Jessi, and they aren't really CITs. They're right next door in 11-B. I think it's a good thing they wound up together and also a good thing I'm not their CIT.

Anyway, as 11-A unpacked, I listened to what was going on around me.

"Oh, my lord!" exclaimed Rachel. "A spider! There's a spider. It's over there on that wall by the knothole. Someone kill it! Quick!"

"How can you see that spider from all the way across the cabin?" asked Freddie. "That's amazing."

"I have bionic vision," replied Rachel. "Honestly I do. For real. You know how, like, normal eyesight is twenty-twenty? And poor eyesight could be, like, two hundred-twenty? Well, mine's twenty-fifteen. That means I can see from twenty feet what most people can only see from fifteen feet. Or something like that. I could have all those numbers mixed up. I really could. But the main thing is, my eyesight's incredible. Once I was — Aughh! Aughh! The spider's moving! Honestly. Someone get rid of it. Please!"

Rachel was inciting mayhem. A couple of girls let out little shrieks. I'm not fond of spiders, but I tried to stay calm. Shari threw a sneaker at the wall, which missed the spider by a mile. The shoe landed on Heather's head. Heather appeared not to notice, and Donna giggled at her.

"Hey, everyone," said Freddie, "the spider's heading for the knothole. I think it's going to crawl outside."

"Smart spider," I said.

"That knothole goes all the way through the wall to the outside?" squeaked Rachel. "Then the spider could come back *in*. Plus we're going to freeze at night."

"Well, the cabins aren't exactly heated, anyway," Charlene pointed out. "And you Mooseheads have your lovely moose sweaters to wear if we have cold weather."

Everyone laughed. Even Heather. Are "ha-ha" words? If so, then I counted wrong. Heather spoke three times this afternoon.

"My boyfriend," said Caryn, "told me the cabins on the other side of the lake are equipped with heating *and* air-conditioning."

"He's lying," said Donna. "They've only got microwaves."

"Who's your boyfriend?" asked Freddie.

"He better not be lying," replied Caryn, "and my boyfriend is Steve Heineman."

"Do you have a boyfriend, Heather?" Shari asked suddenly.

We had pretty much finished our unpacking and were just sitting around our cabin, mostly on the top bunks, since it's so hard to see from the bottom ones. It's like being in a cave. But Heather was lying on her bottom bunk. She was in the journal-writing phase of the afternoon. I looked at her thoughtfully. She reminded me an awful lot of Mallory. In a good way.

"No," said Heather. "I don't have a boyfriend." (Okay, she said four things this afternoon.)

Shari giggled, but then she began to tell one of her unrepeatable jokes, so I wasn't sure whether she was laughing at Heather, or at the punchline she knew was coming up.

After four of Shari's jokes, Charlene said, "Anyone who wants to go exploring now is allowed to. Free afternoon. Go check out the stables, the lake, anything."

I thought Cabin 11-A would come crashing down as everyone jumped off of the top bunk beds and ran to the door. Charlene and Amy followed the campers outside. But I hung back. Heather was still lying on her bunk, writing.

"Aren't you going out?" I asked her.

Heather shook her head solemnly. "Charlene

said anyone who *wants* to go, can go. I don't want to go. I'd rather stay here."

"Why did you come to camp, Heather?" I couldn't resist asking.

"Because my parents made me. They thought it would be a good experience." (Broadening, probably.)

"And what do you think?"

"I'm willing to experiment." Heather looked back at her journal. (So she said quite a few things this afternoon. So I was exaggerating before, okay?)

"Are you sure you don't want to come outside? I'll walk around with you," I offered.

"That's okay," said Heather. "Really. Thanks, but you go ahead."

So I did. I thought a lot about Heather that afternoon.

CHAPTER 7

Saturday night

Dear Laine,

How's New York? Are you surprised to hear that I miss you
and it already? Well, I do. There
is absolutely no use for credit
cards up here. What we could
use is a hospital. Did you know
that six-year-olds get sick a lot?
I don't know why I didn't realize
it before, what with all the baby-
sitting I do. I guess I've just
never spent so much time with
so many six-year-olds. Also,
six-year-olds are loud. I will have
to demonstrate the difference
between "indoor voices" and
"outdoor voices" to them.

Love,
Your frazzled friend,
Stacey

Laine Cummings

The Dakota

72nd and Central Park West

New York, NY 10023

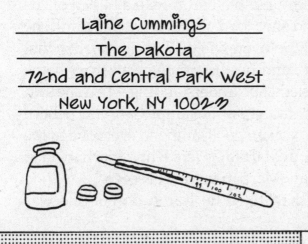

Okay, you guys, I've read your notebook entries, so I know how your afternoons went. There were a few differences between yours and mine. For one thing, *your* campers could unpack for themselves. Mine couldn't. They need a lot more help with everything. I guess that's to be expected.

Barbara, our counselor, Joanne, the other CIT in our cabin, and I went from bunk to bunk, helping the little kids unpack. It seemed that each time we got to a new kid, we got to a new illness, too.

Yuck. I cannot stand sickness, maybe because of my diabetes, and because I've spent a fair amount of time in hospitals over the past few years. So I started off by helping Karen Brewer unpack. I've known Karen since our family moved to Stoneybrook, and Karen is usually healthy.

Today I discovered something new, though. She may be healthy, but put her in with a bunch of six-year-olds and she's loud. Shrill, actually. I think she just gets a little overexcited. Plus, it was her first day at camp, and her first time away from home alone. So I tried to be understanding when she said (shrieked), "Stacey! I'm at camp! Can you believe it? Hey look, you guys." (Calling to everyone in the cabin.) "I'm a Martian. Here's my Martian face. And here's my Martian voice. Eeeeeeee!"

Whoa. I had to settle Karen down. She was

giving me a headache. And she was exciting the other kids. "Would you do me a big favor?" I said to Karen. "Would you be my helper, and go to each camper and make sure she's got everything she came with? If anything's missing, report back to me immediately."

Karen grinned proudly and was off and running.

I moved on to the next camper. "I have a sore throat," she said.

"Hey, Stacey," called Barbara, the counselor, from across the cabin. "Do you know what pink-eye looks like?"

Oh, for gosh sakes. I dashed over to Barbara and looked into the pixie face of a smiling red-head. She didn't seem sick at all. But one eye was about the color of her hair.

"Does it itch?" I asked her.

"Mm-hmm," she said, reaching for her eye.

I pulled her hand back. "Don't touch it," I said. "That'll make it worse." (I sounded exactly like my mother.)

"And now," spoke up a little voice behind me, "you better wash your hand, Shtashey."

I turned around to see who the lisper was. Standing with her hands on her hips and brown hair flowing down her back (her hair was so long she could sit on it) was a sassy-looking camper.

"Why, Nonie?" I asked, pleased with myself for remembering her name.

"A-cause if Valerie'sh hand hash touched her eye, then she hash pinkeye on her hand, sho now you probly have pinkeye on *your* hand and if *you* touch *your* eye *you'll* get pinkeye, too."

Great. Just great, I thought.

"You sure know a lot about pinkeye," I said to Nonie.

"I have three shishters and a brother," she replied. "We've all gone to Camp Moosehead. I know everything about big familiesh, everything about pashing shicknishesh around, and *everything* about camp. You got a queshtion, I can ansher it. Oh, yeah. One more thing. I know everything about playing jokesh on people, too." Nonie looked meaningfully at the other little girls.

"Everything?" repeated Karen.

"Everything."

"I've got two big stepbrothers," Karen told Nonie, "and one of them — his name his Sam — well, *he* knows everything about playing jokes. He's an expert."

"Maybe, maybe not," replied Nonie.

Karen and Nonie became involved in a joke-playing discussion.

I became involved in worrying. In our cabin, we had a sore throat. We had pinkeye. However, the camp does have an infirmary. It's here to fix sore throats and pinkeye. So Barbara walked Valerie and Monique (the girl with the sore throat) over to the infirmary. She left Joanne and me in charge of the rest of the campers.

My worrying continued. Nonie was still telling practical-joke stories. "Hot Shtuff Chewing Gum," she was saying. "It burnsh your mouth out! And once my oldesht shishter, when she wash here at camp, she took her bunkie'sh underwear and ran it up the flagpole!"

The campers giggled delightedly.

But all I could think of was Betsy Sobak. She's the kid Claudia sat for who was the champion practical joker of the world and ended up pulling a trick that landed Claud in the hospital with a broken leg.

The afternoon wore on. Barbara returned with Valerie and Monique, ointment for Valerie's eye, which thankfully wasn't pinkeye, lozenges for Monique's throat, and instructions to watch both girls closely to make sure they didn't get any worse.

Dinnertime. I could feel butterflies in my stomach. Not because I was nervous about eating in a mess hall, or about helping to preside over six-year-olds as *they* ate in a mess hall, but because of the food. I didn't expect it to be good, of course. School cafeteria food never is, so why should mess hall food be any different? It's hard to maintain quality when you're cooking for hundreds. You probably have to cut corners here and there in order to get vats of soup instead of just one pot.

No, I was worried about my diet. Mom and Dad had had three chats with Mrs. Means before camp started. They had told her what I can and can't eat, and that I have to take in a certain number of calories every day. Therefore, if part of the meal is something with sugar or syrup in it, I can't eat it, but I can't skip it, either. I need something nonsugary to replace it.

Mrs. Means said about seventy-five times that she'd see that I was given only meals I could eat. After all, no one wanted to see me go into insulin shock.

So imagine my surprise this evening when I sat down to a meal of meat loaf, carrots, a candied sweet potato, and a honeyed biscuit. The meat and carrots were fine. The potato and the biscuit weren't.

Now what? I couldn't eat just the meat and carrots. That wasn't enough, and besides, I'm supposed to have *extremely* balanced meals. I tried to catch Claudia's eye across the room, but that was impossible. She was busy with her group of kids, and in between us were a bunch of slaphappy, first-day campers. They were shouting, jumping in and out of their seats, and throwing food around. One girl tossed a honeyed biscuit in the air — and I never saw it come down, although it must have eventually.

With a huge sigh, I excused myself from the table and carried my plate into the kitchen.

I nearly crashed into a cook.

"What are you doing in here?" he demanded.

"I can't eat some of these things," I told him.

"Listen," he replied, "you get what you get. I know the food's not gourmet, but you don't see anyone else coming back here just because this isn't like home cooking."

"But I'm diabetic." I was trying to explain what that meant when Mrs. Means came in. She and the cook and I had a talk. When I left the kitchen a little while later, I was carrying a plate of meat, carrots, an apple, and a sugar-free whole-wheat muffin — on a clean plate, with no traces of honey.

Mrs. Means assured me there would be no further problems, but I still had to face my campers, their questions, and a lot of stares.

"How come you get shpecial food, Shtashey?" asked you-know-who.

"I want an apple, too," said Monique. But she couldn't have one. They were for tomorrow's lunch, and there had to be enough to go around. I felt awful.

Somehow, though, we made it through dinner. It was time for a group sing that was to be held in Moosehead Meadow around the flagpole. Mrs. Means had said earlier that it was a nice way to get all the campers together, but I think it was really just an opportunity for her to make a bunch of announcements to us. She did that first. *Then* we got to sing.

The announcements were pretty much what I expected. She reminded us about camp rules and safety measures. Then she started in on health hazards, which didn't thrill me, what with Monique's sore throat. She warned us of poison ivy and poison oak, about not eating mushrooms and berries, and that sort of thing. She added that there were no snakes in the lake — and I heard both Mary Anne and Jessi scream at the very thought of snakes!

Then Mrs. Means told us about something called Lyme disease. "You get it from ticks," she told us. "Not the larger ticks you often see on dogs or cats, but tiny ticks — about the size of the period at the end of a sentence, so they're very hard to see. It's easy to pick up the ticks in woods or fields, or from animals. Lyme disease can be serious, so check yourselves carefully for ticks. And if you notice a round, red, spreading rash anywhere on your body, or begin to feel achy and tired, like you have the flu, go to the infirmary at once."

I was scared to death.

I was also tired and cold and getting bitten by mosquitoes, so I moved back to the edge of the crowd of campers and settled into a comfortable patch of leaves. Maybe the mosquitoes would leave me alone there.

Mrs. Means began the first song. *"Oh, it ain't gonna rain no more, no more. It ain't gonna rain no more. How in the heck can I wash my neck, if it ain't gonna rain no more?"*

Funny song. I grinned and settled into my leafy nest. Maybe camp wouldn't be so bad after all.

CHAPTER 8

Sunday

Dear Claire,

Hi, there! How does it feel to be an only child? You have Mommy and Daddy and the hamster all to yourself. Do you miss your brothers and sisters? I miss you. Camp is fun. We live in cabins. We sleep in bunk beds, just like the ones in the boys' room at home. Last night all the campers gathered at a place called Moosehead Meadow and sang songs. We learned a funny one about someone who couldn't wash their neck because there was no rainwater! Maybe next year you'll come to Camp Moosehead, too.

I love you.

Your sister,
Mallory

Claire Pike

134 Slate Street

Stoneybrook, CT 06800

It was funny to wake up this morning in a tiny bed that wasn't mine, and to know that Jessi was in the bed below me. I turned over and gazed at the things on the three shelves lining my bunk. Then I turned over again and faced out into our cabin. My bunkies were starting to wake up. They stirred in that last, light sleep of the morning, or coughed, or murmured things that were probably the ends of dreams.

I looked at my watch. It read 6:45. We would be awakened at seven. How, I didn't know. I was pretty sure it wouldn't be a camp-sized alarm clock.

I leaned over my bed and peered down at Jessi. She was lying on her stomach, reading *Misty of Chincoteague* for about the eighteenth time.

"PSST!" I hissed. "Jessi!"

Jessi rolled over and looked up at me. She grinned. "Morning."

"Morning," I replied.

"SHHHHHHH!" said someone else. "We've still got fifteen minutes."

Sheesh, I thought. Jessi and I can't do anything right.

I shrugged at Jessi and pulled myself back up to the top bunk, where I opened my copy of *Stormy, Misty's Foal* and began reading *that* for about the eighteenth time.

I was at a really exciting part of the story when:

76

"ATTENTION, ALL CAMPERS AND COUN-SELORS! ATTENTION, ALL CAMPERS AND COUNSELORS! GOOD MORNING. TODAY IS SUNDAY." (Duh.) "BREAKFAST WILL BE SERVED IN HALF AN HOUR. THE MENU IS WAFFLES, BACON, AND ORANGE JUICE. HAVE A NICE DAY!"

I pictured Mrs. Means wearing a smiley face.

Since Jessi and I had been awake for awhile, we immediately snapped our books shut and pulled fresh outfits off of our shelves. I jumped down from my bed, and Jessi and I began to change our clothes.

"The twins are at it again," I heard someone in an upper bunk whisper to someone in a lower bunk. I think it was Mary to Mary.

"Yeah, goody-two-shoes," added Mandi sleepily.

"Can it," said Autumn, from behind her curtain.

I looked around. Jessi and I were the only ones up and moving.

"But there's just a half an hour until breakfast," I whispered nervously to Jessi. "We don't want to be late."

One of the Marys snorted. (How had she even heard me?)

Jessi linked arms with me. "Let's go," she said

resolutely, and we headed to the bathrooms to wash our faces and brush our teeth.

"Oreos," Maureen said as we left the cabin.

I didn't know what she meant, but I did hear Autumn say sharply, "Maureen, I don't want to hear you say that again. Not ever."

"Oreos?" I repeated to Jessi.

Jessi scowled. "Yeah, a really nice word," she said sarcastically, "meaning someone whose skin is Black, but who acts like a white person. Get it? Black on the outside, white on the inside, like an Oreo cookie."

I couldn't believe Maureen would say something so nasty to Jessi. I felt hurt by being teased, but I knew Jessi probably felt much, much worse.

"But Maureen said Oreos," I pointed out. "I'm not Black."

"I know. Either she's really stupid," (I giggled), "or she meant that somehow you and I together make up an Oreo cookie because we stick together so much," said Jessi.

"An Oreo cookie with one cookie part gone because my brother Nicky has bitten it off, dunked it in milk, and eaten it," I said.

Jessi and I laughed at that, and also at Maureen for not even knowing what an Oreo is. She tried to insult us and she used the word all wrong. We were in pretty good moods by the time the rest of our bunkies dragged themselves into the bathrooms.

"There are the twins," said Mary Travis loudly.

"Where?" I replied.

Mary just stared.

"Oh, *us*?" I asked. "I thought you guys said yesterday that we don't look enough alike to be twins."

Mary blushed, then turned on the water in one of the sinks and began washing her face. No one else said anything to Jessi or me, so we left.

We were on our own.

Now maybe this sounds like we were headed for a bad day. Nope. Not at all. We were headed for a fun and funny day.

That was because later, Jessi and I had our first chance to work with the eight-year-olds on their dance routine for Parents' Day. Until we met the kids, we weren't sure whether we were getting Cabin 8-A or Cabin 8-B. We got Cabin 8-B, the cabin with Becca and Charlotte in it!

Oh, boy. First of all, both of them have terrible stage fright, especially Becca. Secondly, Becca has never danced in her life. She has two left feet. How Jessi can be so talented and coordinated, and Becca so untalented and uncoordinated, is beyond me, but that's the way things are. Thirdly, Charlotte is homesick and cries a lot.

(I know this doesn't sound like much fun, but as usual, I'm getting ahead of myself.)

Early Sunday afternoon, Jessi and I walked over to the recreation hall, where we were supposed to meet the girls of 8-B. The rec hall is a large (wooden) building that is empty except for a Ping-Pong table and an air hockey game. The rest of it is used for watching movies or playing games on rainy days, for parties, for dances for the CITs and counselors, and for rehearsals. That's what Autumn told us.

The eight-year-olds arrived at the rec hall just as we did.

"Jessi, Jessi, Jessi!" cried Becca, and flung herself at her sister.

"Mal, Mal, Mal!" cried Charlotte, and flung herself at me. I'm sure she really wanted Stacey, but I was a good second choice.

Jessi and I and the six kids walked into the rec hall. The kids sat on the floor. Jessi and I stood in front of them. I looked helplessly at Jessi. What were we supposed to do? I've never been a teacher. And what I know about dancing you could fit in a thimble.

But Jessi just said easily, "Hi, I'm Jessi Ramsey. I'm Becca's sister. And this is my friend Mallory.

Guess what. You guys have a really important job. You're going to perform a dance on Parents' Day. Don't worry if you think you can't dance. We'll teach you. I've taken lots of ballet lessons. Besides, anyone can dance. It's just another way of expressing yourselves, like talking."

"Jessi dances on *toe*," Becca spoke up importantly. "She's been *in* ballets *on* stage in front of hundreds of people."

"Oooh," breathed the girls, clearly impressed.

"Now, we're not going to do just ballet," Jessi continued. "It's too hard without ballet shoes. We're going to learn a little jazz and throw some aerobics and acrobatics in, too. It'll be fun, I promise. Lots of jumping around."

"Will an awful lot of people be watching us?" asked Charlotte, wavery-voiced. Becca seemed worried, too.

My heart almost broke. Homesickness and stage fright. What a terrible combination. I sat next to Charlotte on the floor and put my arm around her. "I don't know, Char," I told her. "I honestly don't. For now, let's just try dancing. It'll be fun."

"Okay, everybody. On your feet!" Jessi called cheerfully.

We stood up, Charlotte wiping tears from her eyes.

"Mal, you stay with the kids," Jessi said to me,

"and give them a hand when they need it. Or a foot. I'll stand here and lead things."

That was fine with me.

"Warm-ups!" announced Jessi. "And one and two and three and four. And one and two and three and four." She touched her knees, her toes, her knees again, and then her hips as she counted.

Not one of the kids could get the sequence right. Half of them were touching their knees while the other half were touching their toes. And Charlotte kept putting her hands in the air instead of on her hips.

"Ahem," said Jessi, "let's try something else. Everyone curl into a ball on the floor. Now very slowly uncurl yourselves and stand up. Pretend you're flowers growing."

The girls curled up. Then everyone stood slowly, except for Becca, who shot to her feet.

"*Becca*," complained Jessi.

"I'm a sunflower," said Becca. "Sunflowers grow fast. Don't they?"

"Yes."

"And you always say that a good dancer is creative. So — so I was being creative."

Jessi sighed, then smiled. Becca managed to look both proud and troubled. She knew she was not a good dancer, but she wanted very badly to please her big sister.

The "rehearsal" went on for forty-five minutes. Girls crashed into each other. They fell down. They mixed up their rights and their lefts.

They giggled hysterically, even Charlotte.

So did Jessi and I. We were having a great time. But what on earth were we going to do for our program on Parents' Day?

Sunday afternoon

Dear Mom and Watson,

Boy, am I tired. How did you two ever raise so many children? I think I'll just have one kid when I grow up. Or maybe two. Or three. But no more than five or six. Anyway, why am I tired? Not because I'm in a cabin with six eight-year-old campers, but because I'm in a cabin with Charlotte Johanssen. She is so homesick. I feel really bad for her. I'm not sure she's going to last the two weeks here, although Becca Ramsey will be pretty unhappy if she doesn't. Don't get me wrong. Camp is fun, too. I went swimming in the lake this morning, and I also rode a horse!

Love,
Kristy

The Brewers
1210 McLelland Road
Stoneybrook, CT 06800

I wrote a postcard to Mom and Watson and everything I told them was true. I'm having fun at camp and Charlotte is homesick, but she's even more homesick than I let on. Plus I feel kind of out of it with the other CITs in Cabins 8-B and 8-A. There aren't problems, exactly. The CITs haven't been mean to me. Not at all. They couldn't be nicer. It's just that I'm so different from them. Oh, all right, I'll be honest, it's that I'm exactly their age, but I seem so much younger. That's how I felt compared to Stacey and Claudia when the Babysitters Club first began. And that's how I feel now compared to almost all of the club members. The big difference is that I know my friends so well. I feel comfortable with them. So the difference doesn't matter. But I don't know the CITs.

The CITs are Lauren, Izzie, and Tansy. (Tansy is my co-CIT.) The counselors are Jo and Naomi. Jo is my counselor. Everyone knows Jo. She's the only person at Camp Moosehead with a mohawk. The front half is red and the back half is blue. (Well, they were at first.) The second we got to our cabins Old Meanie showed up and said Jo would have to have her hair cut, because such hair is not fitting for a role model. But Jo said no, absolutely not. She said her hair was *her hair* and she could do whatever she wanted with it. Later, though, she took a shower and the red and blue washed out. It turned out the colors were only sprayed on. Jo is smart. I think she did that on purpose. Now Old Meanie feels like she made Jo tone down her hair, when all Jo wanted in the first place was the mohawk. She didn't care about the colors.

Anyway, back to the CITs. The very first thing Tansy said to me as we were walking from the buses to Cabin 8-B (Charlotte clinging desperately to my hand), was, "My name's Tansy. I know it's a weird name. It means someone who's tenacious. In Middle Latin. I mean, it's the Middle Latin word for tenacious. So I don't mind the name at all. It's an important one."

All I could say was, "I looked my name up in a book once and I couldn't find it." I felt really dumb.

Tansy's reply was, "I need new nail polish."

After we had reached the cabins and unpacked, us four CITs took a break. We sat on the steps out front, leaning against posts so we could face each other. Before anyone had opened her mouth, I could tell how different I was from them. There we were, all wearing the camp shirts and shorts and socks. But Tansy, Lauren, and Izzie were wearing smart-looking white lace-up Adidas on their feet, and I was wearing blue Ponies with

Velcro straps. I almost always wear lace-up running shoes, but just before we left for camp, I saw these Ponies in a shoe store and bought them. I thought they looked really cool.

I guess I was wrong.

Tansy and Lauren were wearing nail polish. I wasn't.

Izzie was wearing lipstick and had pierced ears. I wasn't and didn't.

Tansy, Lauren, and Izzie were wearing eye makeup. I wasn't.

The first words out of Lauren's mouth, after a huge sigh, were, "I miss my boyfriend already."

"Me, too," said Izzie and Tansy with equally huge sighs.

The three of them looked at me.

I paused. Then I said, "I miss Bart."

The girls looked relieved.

"He's a friend of mine," I added, not wanting to lie.

"Your *boy*friend?" asked Lauren.

I shook my head.

Lauren glanced at Izzy, Izzy glanced at Tansy, Tansy glanced at both of them and then looked at me.

"Do you have a real boyfriend?" asked Tansy.

"No. Just some friends who are boys."

"You know," said Izzy, leaning toward me, "you would look so pretty if you cut your hair a little and got rid of your bangs."

As Izzy leaned over, I caught sight of a bra strap peeking out from under the shoulder of her shirt. Oh, lord. Suddenly I was sure Tansy and Lauren were wearing bras, too. I wasn't, of course. Have I ever? Furthermore, I want to point out that I'm the shortest of us CITs. I'm the shortest Babysitters Club member, too. Won't I *ever* grow up?

Well, anyway, soon Tansy, Lauren, and Izzie were all examining me and making comments: "Blush would help." "What other shoes did she bring?" "I think plum nail polish would go best with her eyes."

It was as if I weren't even there; as if I were just a spot on a slide under a microscope. I felt like an amoeba.

I also felt like I was four years old. Was that how Charlotte was feeling?

That night was the group sing, though, and I really had fun. And today, the other CITs and I went swimming and rode horses. In between, however . . .

Charlotte.

Oh, she is a mess. At dinner last night (if you could call it "dinner"), she dropped her fork on the floor. For Charlotte, that was bad enough. She was so embarrassed by that one little incident (and believe me, people were dropping things right and left, so it was no big deal), that by the time she'd found it under our table, she was crying. Then, as she straightened up, practically from out of nowhere came one of those honeyed biscuits. It dropped onto her head from the ceiling! Poor Charlotte.

I took her out of the mess hall to clean her up. When we were finished, she tried to tell me something. But she was crying awfully hard. What I heard was, "I-I-I-I-I-I-wahhhhh g-o-m-e!"

"You want to what?" I said, kneeling down next to her. We were in the bathroom in Mrs. Meanie's office.

"Gome," Char replied. (Hiccup.)

"Gome? Gome? . . . *Oh.* Go home?"

Charlotte nodded.

Mrs. Means let us use her phone. (There are practically no phones here. The only other one is in the infirmary. Plus, there are two phones on the boys' side.)

After Charlotte's mother figured out what "gome" meant, she talked to Charlotte for a long time. At least I think she did, because Charlotte was quiet for a long time. Dr. Johanssen must also have told Charlotte she could call any time she wanted (Charlotte called again an hour later), and that if she really wanted, she *could* come home. I think Charlotte might have done that, except for Becca. She couldn't desert her friend. She did, however, spend the night with me. I mean, literally. In my sleeping bag.

The next morning, Jo was in charge of the campers and that was when she found out everything Charlotte's afraid of. Horses, swimming in the lake, boats . . . Charlotte sort of enjoyed a dance rehearsal with Jessi and Mallory early in the afternoon, but later, she wouldn't agree to anything except archery. This was because no one else wanted to arch (or whatever it's called) and there's no archery instructor anyway. Just some old bows and arrows and targets. Guess who was put in charge of Charlotte? Me. I wanted to go swimming, which was what practically everyone else was doing, but I didn't want to hurt Charlotte's feelings, and besides, as a CIT, watching the campers is my job.

We set up a target in a field that no one was using (since they were all swimming). I showed Charlotte how to put on her wrist guard, how to position the bow and arrow, how to aim, and thought, Good thing we had that dumb archery unit in gym this year.

Charlotte took aim. She pulled the arrow back. She let it fly.

WHOOSH!

As the arrow was heading for the target, a little kid stepped onto the other side of the field. She was headed for the lake, wearing swimming trunks and trying to walk in flippers. Suddenly she tripped and fell.

"Aughhh!" shrieked Charlotte. "Aughhh! Aughhh! I shot her!"

"Char, you did not. The kid's walking away. And, look — you hit the target."

Charlotte wasn't listening to me. Finally I packed everything up, took Char back to our cabin, and began reading *A Morgan for Melinda* to her, which I found on Becca's bunk. It's a horse story. I thought maybe she'd learn not to be afraid of horses. But what I was wondering was whether Char should be at Camp Moosehead at all.

CHAPTER 10

Tuesday

Dear Mom and dad,
    Hi how are you? Me, I'm just fin. Camp is realy fun. I have riden a horse and swam in a lake. But mostly I hav been in the art and crafts cabin. As you can imergine. I am working on potery but also on some riddle work. Tell Mimi now I know why she and Mary Ann like it so much. I hop she teaches me to knit when I com home if she can. Guess what Haly Bradock is teaching her bunkies how to do Sign Langage it was her own idea.
                                            Love,
                                            Claudia

P.S. I met a cute guy, realy cute. And he's Japanese!

Mr. and Mrs. John and Rioko Kishi

58 Bradford CT

Stoneybrook, Conn 06800

Well, I just got finished writing to my parents. I told them about riding and swimming and arts and crafts. I told them about Haley teaching the kids sign language. I didn't tell them that I'm spending my money in the canteen on M&Ms, licorice sticks, Snickers Bars, Almond Joys, etc. I am in seventh heaven. ("Seventh heaven's" something Mom says, but I wonder what it means. I know it means "happy," but . . . where are the other six heavens? Oh, well.)

I also didn't tell my parents the whole story about the boy I met. But let me go back to the beginning of the day first, starting with breakfast. Breakfast was honeyed biscuits left over from Saturday, sunnyside-up eggs that slid around on our plates, and black things that might have been English muffins, but it was hard to tell. The meal was simply gross. So afterward, I ran immediately to the canteen. I was desperate. Sally, the other CIT, and Haley and Vanessa came with me.

We all had money in our pockets, we were starving, and we got there before the canteen opened. My watch read 8:58. The canteen opens at nine. They are very precise.

Two counselors, I think one was Autumn and I *know* the other was Mohawk Jo, were manning the canteen that morning. When they opened the sales window and found the four of us on the other side, practically drooling with hunger, they looked a little startled.

"How was breakfast?" asked Autumn.

Sally pretended to faint and I pretended to have to catch her.

"Food," Sally gasped. "Please. Food. . . . Real food."

"All right," said Jo, "what'll you have?"

"Ring-Dings," answered Sally.

"Peanut butter crackers," replied Vanessa.

"Fake apple pie," said Haley.

"A Snickers Bar, an Almond Joy, a Mars Bar, a bag of Doritos, two packages of Peanut M&Ms, a pack of Twinkies, and some Cheese Doodles." (That was me.)

Jo and Autumn stared.

"How do you stay so thin?" asked Jo.

"And how come your complexion's so good?" asked Autumn.

I shrugged. "Don't know. Just lucky, I guess. Or maybe good genes. I take after my grandmother."

Sally, Vanessa, Haley, and I raced back to our cabin, eating on the way.

"I've never been so hungry in my whole life," said Vanessa, cramming a third cracker into her mouth.

"The food here is terrible," agreed Haley, who

hardly ever complains. "This apple pie is the best thing I've eaten since I got here. I wonder what the boys' food is like," she added, probably thinking about her brother on the other side of the lake.

"Just the same, I bet," said Sally, "but boys never notice a difference. They'd happily eat pond scum and gorilla feet, if they didn't know what it was. Or most of them would."

By the time we reached our cabin, everyone had finished their food but me. That was because I'd bought so much. All I'd eaten was a package of M&Ms. I shoved everything else in a tote bag on one of my shelves. Since I wasn't at home, I didn't have to bother to hide it.

That morning, our cabin went on a horseback ride. It was fun! I haven't spent much time on horses, but this was nice. Of course, the horses weren't like rodeo horses, rearing on their hind legs and jumping around. They just walked along a well-worn path through the woods. Even so, by the time we had gotten back to the stables, brushed the horses, helped muck out their stalls, and learned how to get them ready for the next riders, we were pretty disgusting-looking.

"You have straw in your hair, Claudia!" said Jayme, dancing around like a pixie.

"And you have dust on your nose," I replied, smiling.

"I think *I've* got dust *in* my nose," said Brandy, and sneezed.

When we reached our cabin, I made a beeline for the mirror.

I was worse than a mess, I was a *fright*! There really was straw in my hair. There was also dirt on my face, dust on my clothes and (oh, ew) an inchworm on my shoulder. I took the inchworm off my shoulder and put it on Sally's pillow to see how she'd react.

Then I realized I smelled like horses and manure, but before I could shower I had to get the straw out of my hair.

That's just what I was doing when I heard footsteps on the cabin porch. Heavy footsteps.

"Hello?" called a boy's voice.

"Aughh! Aughh!" Everyone began screaming.

"I'm changing!" cried Leeann.

"I'm naked!" shrieked Vanessa.

"I'm Claudia," I said.

I knew exactly how bad I looked. I knew exactly how bad I smelled. But at least I was dressed.

I had turned away from the mirror (wooden-framed) and stepped outside. A boy was standing on the porch. Two others were behind him on the path. When I came outside, the first boy backed up and joined his friends.

"Hi," he said. "I'm John and these are my

friends." (He pointed to the other boys as he introduced them.) "We're CITs from across the lake. We're here to officially invite . . ."

John kept on talking, but I wasn't listening. All I could do was look at one of the other boys. He was gorgeous. Absolutely gorgeous — and incredible and wonderful. I'm sure of it.

And I think he's Japanese. Anyway, he's Asian. He has black, black hair and dark eyes, and clear skin like mine. His hair is kind of punk. The top part stands straight up. He must have to use mousse or something on it in the morning. That and his black high-top sneakers were about as punk as he could get at Camp Moosehead. The rest of his clothes were of the Moosehead variety.

I gazed at him.

He gazed at me.

John was still talking, but I wasn't listening, and I don't think the gorgeous boy was listening, either. At least not until we heard John say, "Well, see you a week from today."

The next thing I knew, the boys were gone.

"What? What?" I sputtered as I fled into the cabin.

I found my campers, Sally, and Meghan grinning at me.

"Woo — *oo*," said Brandy. "Claud and someone, sitting in a tree, K-I-S-S-I-N-G!"

"First comes love," added Leeann, "then comes —"

"What were they doing here?" I interrupted Leeann.

"What were they *do*ing here?" Sally repeated. "Weren't you listening? They were inviting us to the CIT Movie Night next Tuesday, and the big CIT dance next Wednesday — on the boys' side."

"That boy," I said softly. "I have to meet him. Soon. But I don't even know his name."

"Heyyy," said Vanessa. "You really like him, don't you?"

I nodded.

"Love at first sight," said Haley dreamily.

The campers grew quiet and I realized that *they* had just realized that this was important to me. Very important.

"I've got to see him," I said again. "Before next Tuesday. I can't wait that long. Camp will practically be over by then."

"We'll help you," spoke up Gail, who's our quietest camper. "We'll find him for you somehow."

"Yeah, we know there's a boy across the lake named John. We'll start with him," added Brandy.

"But there must be a thousand Johns over there," Jayme pointed out.

"And there are only two phones here: in the infirmary and in Old Meanie's office. How are we going to get in touch with the boys' side?" wondered Vanessa. (I could tell she liked the idea of a challenge, though.)

"Hey, not to change the subject," Meghan interrupted, and we turned our attention to our counselor, "but Claudia, did you get the rest of John's message?"

"The rest of it?" I repeated, and everyone laughed.

"He and his friends had to go back across the lake, so John asked you and Sally to spread the word about the movie and the dance to the other CITs here. Just tell every CIT you see about them, okay? Word will spread fast."

I nodded. Then I climbed onto my top bunk. I reached for my tote bag, needing junk food badly. I was having an attack. I put my hand in the bag and felt around. Empty!

At that moment I heard two shrieks. One was a shriek of laughter. That came from Vanessa Pike. The other was a shriek of horror. That came from Sally. I scrambled off of my bunk bed, stepping on Sally's hand in the process.

"What's the matter?" I exclaimed.

"There's a worm on my bed!" she cried, and darted across the cabin, out of worm's way. (Oh, so *that's* what would happen if Sally found an inchworm on her pillow.)

Nearby, Vanessa was laughing. I didn't have

to ask her why, since she couldn't wait to tell me. "You know why you can't find your candy?" she managed to say. "Because I hid it!"

This was Vanessa's idea of a big joke. The other campers thought it was pretty funny, too.

Vanessa produced the candy. And I handed it around to everyone in my cabin, which was very generous of me. But to tell the truth, I was so intrigued by John's friend that I, Claudia Kishi, barely even cared about the size of my junk food supply.

CHAPTER 11

Thursday

Dear Dad,

　　Hi! How are you? I'm fine.
Camp's fine. Gotta go.
　　　Bye. Love,
　　　　　Mary Anne

P.S. Pat Tigger
　　　for me.

I felt a little bad. I wrote a postcard to my father this morning, but I didn't have enough time to write a long one. So I wrote him a short one in big handwriting instead. I was too busy for postcards. This is why:

Dear Logan,

I miss you so much! I am counting the days until next Wednesday. This next week will seem like a year. I think of you and want to ~~swon~~ swoon. Or, to feel your arms around me at the dance! It has been too long since our last kiss.

I will be wearing the formal moose wear, of course, and a yellow ribbon in my hair. What of you, my love? Will you wear your after-shave? If you were to bring me a yellow flower to match my ribbon, I would melt in your arms.

Love forever, kisses and hugs,
Your love-bunny.
Mary Anne XXOO

Logan has never in his life called me his love-bunny. I can't even imagine him doing that. And I've certainly never called *him my* love-bunny. We aren't like that.

I wrote that note for one reason only, and it

barely had a thing to do with Logan. Not directly, anyway. I didn't even intend for him to see it. It was written for Randi, my co-CIT, to discover. I wanted her and Faye and Julie, the CITs next-door in 7-B, to read it. (I figured that if Randi saw it, Faye and Julie would hear about it no more than one second later.)

Why did I want the girls to see the note? Because I wanted to prove just how sophisticated I was. I know, I know. It was stupid. And it doesn't even sound like me.

Since when did I care about stuff like that? Since I got to Camp Moosehead and was kind of separated from my friends, that's when.

Anyway, what I did was write that note yesterday and leave it on my bunk, hoping Randi would be the one to find it first — and she was. And, just as I suspected, she raced it over to Faye and Julie. I had taken Margo Pike and Nancy Dawes to the nature cabin to get them ready for this butterfly hunt they wanted to go on the next day. When we returned, Randi, Faye, and Julie were standing in the middle of the cabin, crowded around the note. Their heads snapped up as we entered, but they didn't look guilty, only smug.

"Um, Mary Anne," said Randi, sauntering over to me, "you left this on your bunk. I took it because I didn't want any of the campers to see it. I mean, really, what would they think? 'Love-bunny'? 'Too long since our last kiss'? 'Swonning'?"

Personally, I had a feeling our campers would be much more interested in whether they could sneak up to the windows of Old Meanie's cabin that evening and try to see what was on her TV, but I kept my mouth shut.

"So," said Faye, as the campers changed into their bathing suits (it was almost time for afternoon Open Swim), "how are you going to get this note to Logan?"

"Yeah, do you think you can do it fast enough for him to get you a yellow flower?"

"Maybe you should go at night," spoke up another voice. The CITs and I turned around.

Tara the Terror. *She* was more interested in Logan and me than in Mrs. Means' TV. "But if you go at night," she continued slowly, "you'd have to get around bed-check. Somehow."

I sighed inwardly. Bed-check. I hate it. I think it says Old Meanie doesn't trust us. Imagine her and the head counselors checking each and every bed at night to make sure they're occupied and no one is doing something she shouldn't be doing. Like taking a note around the lake to her boyfriend.

"You can get around bed-check," said Julie. "No problem."

"Why not go tonight?" added Faye. "The sooner the better. You'll want the best yellow flower Logan can find."

I was penned in. I had to go. If I didn't, I'd look like a bigger baby than they already thought I was. But a trip around the lake? Alone? At night? I didn't even know the way. And I was not going to take a boat by myself at night. That would be just plain foolish.

"I feel so silly," I said, "but I don't even know the way to the boys' side."

"Oh, that's a cinch," replied Randi. "There's just this one path. I'll draw a map for you. All you have to do is follow the path around the lake. There aren't even any turn-offs. Of course it'll be pitch black at night, but you've got a flashlight, haven't you?"

I nodded.

"Gosh, it's too bad about Ronald Feenie and Harve 'the Knife' Johnson," Randi continued.

"Who?" I said. "Are they counselors on the boys' side?"

Faye and Julie didn't say anything. They looked at Randi.

"Oh, no," Randi replied. "They're the escapees."

"Escapees?" I gasped. "Escapees from where?"

"That asylum over in Peacham. It's just a small

asylum. But these insane murderers got loose a couple of days ago."

"Oh! Oh, right!" said Julie suddenly. "The ones who killed all those —"

"SHHH!" hissed Faye. "Don't say it. There's no point. I'm sure they're not in this area anyway."

Well, I had no idea whether to believe the girls. They probably weren't telling the truth. They were probably making all that stuff up. Then again, I knew they'd snuck over to Old Meanie's once and watched her television. They'd heard the local news. I hadn't.

Anyway, I didn't think I had much choice. It was either make the nighttime trip, or spend the next week and a half knowing that Randi, Faye, and Julie thought I was a complete and total jerk.

Maybe the trip would help build character. The Camp Moosehead brochure promised to do that.

Besides, it *would* be nice to see Logan.

Bed-check is at nine-thirty every night. I do not understand the logic behind it. No one over seven is remotely tired at that hour. So everyone gets up again after bed-check anyway.

On Wednesday night, I wanted to be out of Cabin 7-A before bed-check. It would have been easier to wait until afterward, but I did *not* want to be wandering around woods infested with murderers at midnight. I wanted to leave as soon as darkness fell. So I pulled the *very* oldest trick in history. I stuffed some clothes and things in my sleeping bag to make it look as if I were inside. Then I placed a large cantaloupe (stolen from the kitchen by Randi) at the head of the sleeping bag and put my pillow over it, as if I were trying to drown out noise.

Everyone except Connie, our counselor, watched me do this. They all knew what was going on. (Connie was at a counselors' meeting over at Mrs. Means'.) The girls watched me put on a sweater, load my flashlight with new batteries, and put the map and that dumb love-bunny note in my pocket.

Randi walked me to the path around the lake. "If you run into Ronald or Harve the Knife, just fall down and play dead," she advised me. "They'll probably lose interest and leave you alone."

Great, just great.

Randi left me, and I set off down the path, the beam from my flashlight bouncing ahead of me. I prayed that the batteries in the flashlight were in good working order and hadn't been sitting in the hardware store for five years before I bought them.

Crunch, crunch, crunch. I kept stepping on twigs and leaves as I walked along. *Swoosh, swoosh,*

swoosh. The water from the lake lapped at the shore nearby. I wished my trip could be quieter. But it only seemed to get noisier. An owl hooted. Crickets chirped.

I shivered.

I don't know how long I'd been walking when I heard a voice say softly, "There she is." It was a man's voice.

There was a pause. Then another voice said, "That's not her."

"Yes, it is. It must be. I see a light."

I couldn't help it. I forgot what Randi had said about playing dead. Instead I began to scream.

"Go away! Get out! Don't kill me! I've got a kitten at home. He needs me. Oh, yeah. I've also got a gun."

"Mary Anne?"

Aughh! How did the escaped murderers know my name?

Then I heard another voice. This time it was a woman's. "Mary Anne. We know you're there. Stay where you are, okay?"

The voice sounded familiar but . . . maybe there was a third mental-asylum escapee, someone the police didn't know about with a name like Bonnie "the Hatchet" Jones or Goldie "Fast-Finger" Swordman.

"Mary Anne!" the voice called again. "It's me, Connie."

Connie!

"Connie!" I finally replied. "I'm here!" I wasn't lost, but I have to admit I was relieved to be found, even if I was going to be in trouble.

I stood where I was, flashlight on, and was soon surrounded by Connie, Mrs. Means, and two guys who were probably counselors at Logan's camp. (They were wearing moose sweat shirts.)

Mrs. Means frowned and looked disappointed, but Connie hugged me. "I was so worried about you!" she cried.

"How did you know I was gone — and where to look for me?" I asked.

"Tara told Mrs. Means during bed-check that you hadn't been feeling well. When we looked in on you we found the cantaloupe. Then the story just sort of came out. Tara couldn't help herself."

Connie didn't look any too pleased with Tara, which delighted me.

Then Mrs. Means said that I would have to be punished. This was my punishment: no swimming for three days. What a tragedy.

One of the boy counselors made me hand over my note to Logan. "We'll see that he gets it," he said. His voice was sort of strained. Was he making a threat or a promise? I couldn't tell. And I nearly panicked. That note! That wasn't the kind of thing I'd *ever* send to Logan. What would he think when he read it? That I'd gone crazy? That I was more serious about our relationship than he thought? Oh, no. Oh, no. It was too horrible to think about.

Mrs. Means spoke to the boys. Then they walked off down the path. Connie, Old Meanie, and I turned around and walked back the way I had come. Nobody said a word the whole way. I was dying to ask whether there really were some escaped lunatics, but I didn't think this was the right time for it. Also, I was beginning to wonder what to expect from Randi, Faye, and Julie when we reached the cabin. On the one hand, I hadn't made it to Logan. On the other hand, it hadn't been my fault. The Terror, one of our own campers, had ruined the adventure (thank goodness).

Mrs. Means left us when we got to her cabin. Before she went inside, she gave me a *look* and warned me never to try something like that again, young lady. (Now I see how she got her nickname.) Under ordinary circumstances, I might have cried then, since I was in trouble and I'm not used to being in trouble, but as soon as Old

Meanie had disappeared, Connie put her arm around me again.

"I tried to sneak around the lake once," she told me.

"You did?"

"Mm-hmm. To see a boy. When I was a CIT."

I smiled into the darkness.

Back at 7-A, we found a few lights on and everyone awake. Connie went next door to talk to the 7-B counselor, and Faye and Julie tiptoed over and joined Randi and me in a huddle on Randi's bunk. The campers watched us solemnly from their own bunks, even Tara, which I thought was odd. Why wasn't she gloating?

For a few seconds the other CITs just stared at me.

"Okay, so I didn't make it," I said crossly. "So sue me."

Faye and Julie continued to stare, mouths slightly open, but Randi whispered, "How far did you get?"

"How far around the lake? I don't know. About halfway, I guess," I replied.

"*Halfway?* You know, only two other girl CITs have ever tried to sneak around the lake," said Randi. "In the whole history of Camp Moosehead."

So that's why Tara wasn't gloating. She was as awed as Randi. So were the other campers. So were Faye and Julie. I couldn't believe it.

I grinned and shrugged my shoulders. "Nothing to it," I said. "If Tara hadn't tattled," (here was my chance to give Tara a *look* of my own), "I'd have made it all the way around."

Tara actually seemed slightly ashamed.

I knew I wouldn't have to worry about impressing the CITs anymore, no matter how I dressed.

"You know what was weird, though?" I went on. "The counselors from the boys' side took my note and said they'd give it to Logan for me. They said it right in front of Old Meanie. I was surprised. I thought Old Meanie would have torn it up or something. As punishment. Not let it get to Logan."

"Hmm," said Randi, "I wonder what that means."

I wondered, too. And I didn't find out for a while.

CHAPTER 12

FRIDAY

DEAR MOM AND DAD,

HI. HOW ARE YOU? I'M FINE. CAMP MOOSEHEAD IS FINE, TOO. MOST OF THE TIME. I MEAN, YOU KNOW — POISON IVY, CAMP FOOD, DUMB RULES. BUT I LEARNED HOW TO CANOE AND I SWAM TO THE MIDDLE OF THE LAKE AND BACK, WHICH EARNED ME A BADGE THAT MEANS I CAN DO ANY WATER SPORT ANY TIME I WANT. I MIGHT LEARN TO WATER-SKI.

LOVE

LOGAN

MR. AND MRS. BRUNO

689 BURNT HILL ROAD

STONEYBROOK, CT 06800

Stacey said I have to write some entries for her dumb book, and mail them to her in New York when camp's over. I have never kept a diary or a notebook, except for one week after I read *The Diary of Anne Frank*, and that was for an English assignment. But Stacey wants Camp Moosehead views for her book from every club member who was there this summer, and that includes me. Okay, here I go.

First off, I want to say that I wrote my parents a postcard today, making it sound like water sports are the biggest thing in my life right now. What a lie. Getting my badge *was* exciting, but the postcard doesn't begin to tell the story of what's going on over here on the boys' side of camp.

I was assigned to Cabin 7-A. (The cabin names here are *so* thought-provoking.) And guess who three of my campers are — Jackie Rodowsky, Buddy Barrett, and Matt Braddock. Matt was assigned to my cabin because the counselor and I know enough sign language to be able to communicate with him. And Buddy pretty much knows sign language, too, because he's Matt's friend.

Matt and Buddy are fine as campers. . . . Then there's Jackie. I'm exhausted after baby-sitting with him for just an hour. Imagine sharing a cabin with him for two weeks. The weirdest things have happened. Bunks have collapsed. (No one was hurt.) The door is permanently stuck three inches open. (Mosquitoes, mosquitoes, mosquitoes.) And dried toothpaste is all over the floor. I think Jackie dropped his tube and then stepped on it.

Our other campers are Curtis, who's teaching the kids to play poker; Russell, who spends his days writing poetry to a camper in 8-B over on the girls' side; and Thomas, who likes to be called simply T. Overall, the campers are a good bunch, except for when Jackie goes on a disaster spree. It's the CITs (not including me) that I really worry about. They act as though they were just let out of prison. Well, we *were* all just let out of school. But even so.

They are hard to keep up with.

The other CIT in my cabin is Rick. He is wild. Mr. Meanie, the camp director over here (husband of Old Meanie), lets him get away with wearing a flowered Hawaiian shirt over his camp shirt. Henry and Cliff, the CITs next door in 7-B, are never without sunglasses, and spend most of their time working on their tans, spying on the Meanies when Old Meanie comes to visit, and trying to figure out how to switch movies and get a scary one for Movie Night.

It's important to know all this before I describe what happened at lunch today. I was sitting at Table 7 (whoa, thought-provoking) with the twelve campers, our two counselors, and us four CITs. We CITs were crowded together at one end of the table discussing whether we thought the Meanies ever watched anything besides old Doris Day movies on Mr. Meanie's TV, when another counselor (Meanie's personal assistant, I think) handed me a note.

"From your girlfriend across the lake," he said, and walked away.

My girlfriend? This must have been some kind of joke. One of Rick's, maybe. Or else, maybe Mary Anne really had sent me a note. Either way, I was in for it. I knew that right off.

Sure enough, Cliff made a grab for the paper, but I pulled it away. I am pretty quick. I skimmed the note.

So did Cliff. He was reading it over my shoulder, only I didn't know that until it was too late.

"'Love-bunny'?!" hooted Cliff. And then, "'*After*-shave'?"

"What about after-shave?" said Rick.

"Who's that from?" asked Henry. "Wait. Is that from the girl who tried to sneak over here with a note last night and didn't make it? I heard about that. She left a watermelon under her pillow to make it look like she was there at bed-check. A *watermelon.* . . . That girl was coming to see *you*, Logan?"

"I guess so," I said.

"Boy, I never thought I'd get to see the actual note," Henry went on.

"Allow me to read it to you," said Cliff, taking it from me because I let him. (The story was out. I was licked.) "I believe you will find it highly entertaining." Cliff snapped the paper in front of him and cleared his throat. Everyone at our table tuned in for the reading.

Cliff did a pretty good job. In a high, squeaky voice, he read every word from "Dear Logan, I miss you so much!" to "Your love-bunny, Mary Anne XXOO."

I had never been so embarrassed in my life. I had also never been so touched. I figured the Meanies had made sure I got the note at lunch-time so that everyone would see it, and that this was some sort of punishment for Mary Anne or me or both of us. But this was the first note I'd ever gotten from Mary Anne that didn't just say, "Happy birthday," or "Meet me at my locker after sixth period."

Does she really mean those things? I was wondering. Does she really want a yellow —

At that point I realized that absolutely everyone at my table was laughing. They were laughing so hard that Henry and Cliff steamed up their shades and had to take them off. And Jackie Rodowsky choked, knocked over his milk, and then fell out of his chair.

I took a long look at Cliff. Then, very slowly, I loaded my spoon with peas and topped them off with creamed corn. I aimed the spoon at him.

"No way, man," said Cliff, pushing his chair back.

I boinged the spoon in his direction anyway. The peas and corn got him on the forehead. It was a good thing he'd taken his sunglasses off.

Cliff ripped a muffin in half, buttered it, and threw it at me. It missed and hit a kid at the table behind me. Quick as a flash, the kid sucked Coke into his straw and sprayed it over at us. Someone else thought that was a pretty good idea and tried it at his table.

Pandemonium.

Food was flying everywhere. Stuff landed on the ceiling and dripped gooily onto our heads. Milk and Coke shot across the mess hall in arcs. (Jackie Rodowsky sat on a peanut butter-and-jelly sandwich, but that might have been an accident.) Mr. Meanie stood up to yell at us and a glob of pickle relish splatted onto the moose head on his shirt. When he blew his whistle, mustard squirted out.

By that afternoon, I was in trouble, which shouldn't surprise anyone. Mr. Meanie's punishment? I was banned from arts and crafts for three days. What a tragedy.

Rick, Henry, and Cliff looked at me with a little more respect. And my counselor confessed that he had once started a food fight, too.

Now — I better put this notebook of mine away before someone catches me keeping a diary. That would ruin any respect I earned today.

CHAPTER 13

Sunday,

Dear Mom,

Guess what — our cabin is going on an overnight camping trip! I can't wait. Remember when I did that at Camp La Brea in California? Charlene (she's our counselor) and Amy (the other CIT) and I will be in charge. We have a group of six eleven-year-olds, so it shouldn't be too difficult. The campers are really excited, too. We're busy packing and planning and trying to think of all our scariest ghost stories.

See you in less than a week!

Love,
Dawn

Mrs. Sharon Schafer

177 Burnt Hill Road

Stoneybrook, CT

06800

The eleven-year-old campers are the only ones who get to go on an overnight. We go one night, 11-B goes the next night. The trip will be a blast. The food won't be too healthy, but I can't wait for a night under the stars and all that tramping through the woods and nature stuff.

The last week has been great, especially the past couple of days, as our campers become more and more excited about their adventure. They've written and rewritten lists of stuff to bring. They've also started packing their knapsacks, but they always put stuff in them that they'll need before they leave, and then they have to unpack. I've seen them put in everything from underwear to an electric toothbrush. (Freddie put the toothbrush in; Heather pointed out its uselessness.)

Speaking of Heather, she hasn't changed a bit. The other campers think she's weird, so she wasn't too popular when she corrected Freddie's mistake. I just don't understand Heather. She's always pleasant when she says anything. But she speaks so rarely. She reads and writes and sometimes goes to arts and crafts or the nature cabin or quiet places like that. She never goes to the lake for Open Swim, and once she cut her mandatory swimming lesson. I found her in her bunk reading *The Grey King*, by Susan Cooper. She knew she'd missed her lesson, and didn't care. But she wasn't rude about it. The best word I can think of to describe Heather is *inscrutable*, which was on one of my vocabulary lists this year.

The first few days of camp, the other kids tried to be nice to Heather, but she wouldn't or couldn't come out of her shell. She never stopped reading and writing and not participating. Now the girls either tease her or ignore her. I think their feelings are hurt, especially Rachel's. Rachel tries so hard to be friendly to everyone, and she doesn't understand when someone isn't friendly back.

Here is a typical evening in my cabin after bed-check (when the lights are supposed to be off). Slowly flashlights come on. Charlene draws the curtain around her bed and pretends not to notice the flashlights. Shari burps loudly and everyone laughs. (Shari can burp on command.) Everyone laughs, that is, except Heather. She has propped her flashlight on a book and is writing furiously in her journal.

Shari directs another — louder — burp in Heather's direction. I don't think Heather even hears it because she's concentrating so hard, but Donna, from below Shari, says, "Never mind. She's ignoring us again. The best thing to do is give her nothing to ignore. Ignore her back."

"What a baby," says Freddie.

"What a bore," says Caryn.

"That's enough," Charlene finally calls from behind her curtain.

The campers are quiet for about two minutes. Then Rachel leans over the side of her bunk and says, "Psst! Heather! Hey, Heather!"

"Hmm?" replies Heather distractedly.

Rachel drops her voice so Charlene won't hear her. "Want to sneak over to Old Meanie's with us and watch TV?"

Heather finally looks up. She smiles. Rachel smiles back. "No," replies Heather, "but thanks. Really. I just want to stay here."

"Why are you even talking to her?" Caryn asks Rachel.

Rachel shrugs. Heather returns to her journal. The girls decide not to go to Old Meanie's. And none of them speaks to Heather until the next morning.

Very typical. I feel sorry for Heather, but she doesn't seem to want to change. The girls gave her openings and opportunities, and she ignored them. So now the girls ignore Heather.

At the moment, it is Sunday night, the night before we leave for the big camping trip. And earlier, something awful happened. It was seven o'clock. We had just come back to our cabin after supper, which was gross, and were getting ready to have a marathon Monopoly game with 11-B, since the weather was drizzly. Otherwise, we would have had to go to Moosehead's outdoor amphitheater for an astronomy talk by the nature counselor. After that, we would have watched for falling stars. Frankly, every camper was glad it was raining.

We had just gotten together the Monopoly set and a supply of popcorn and potato chips and were heading for 11-B, when the door to 11-A opened and Mrs. Means strode in. We stopped in our tracks, even though we weren't doing anything wrong. Rachel dropped a bowl of popcorn.

We were surprised that Mrs. Means ignored that, but she did. "Charlene," she said, "I need to talk to you."

I knew we were all thinking, Ooh, Charlene's in trouble, but we liked her too much to have said anything.

"Let's go to your sleeping area," said Mrs. Means quietly. She took Charlene by the arm, led her to the bed, and drew the curtain around them. Amy and the campers and I didn't budge. We just stared at each other. We knew we should leave Charlene and Mrs. Means alone, or at least clean up the popcorn, but we couldn't move. This sounded really serious.

From behind the curtain we could hear the

low murmur of voices. Then we heard Charlene begin to cry. A few minutes later, Mrs. Means moved the curtain aside and stepped out, leaving Charlene by herself.

"Girls?" she said. (We gathered around her.) "I'm afraid there's been some bad news. Charlene's mother is very sick and Charlene has to go home right away. Her older brother will be picking her up in a couple of hours."

"Oh, no!" I couldn't help crying out. I made a move toward the curtain.

But Mrs. Means stopped me. "Not yet," she said. "Give her some time to herself. Later you can help her pack her things."

"Okay," I replied, drawing back.

"But what about a counselor for our cabin?" asked Donna, and we all knew that what she was really asking was, "Will we still be able to go on our overnight tomorrow?"

"Don't worry," Mrs. Means replied. "I've got a list of people who are available as replacement counselors this summer. Most of them were former CITs here, so they're familiar with the camp. I promise that you'll have a new counselor tomorrow and that all your activities will go as planned. Meanwhile, Dawn, you're in charge after Charlene leaves." Mrs. Means looked at Amy. "That's just because Dawn has had more camping experience than you have. No other reason. You'll be her righthand CIT."

Amy nodded. Nobody felt like arguing about anything. We were all too stunned by the changes and surprises (even if we did feel relieved about our overnight), and we felt too bad for Charlene.

Mrs. Means went next door then to talk to the 11-B counselor. The campers and Amy and I cleaned up the popcorn silently. Caryn took the Monopoly board over to 11-B and left it there. When she came back, we put away the evening's junk food and lay around on our bunks, reading and doing other Heather-type things.

Charlene left two hours later. We all hugged her good-bye and cried, even Heather.

"Good-bye, Charlene!" we called, as her brother's car drove off. "We hope your mom gets better! Really soon!"

"We'll miss you!" I added.

We filed back into 11-A, damp from the rain, and as gloomy as Winnie-the-Pooh's friend Eeyore. I had to do something. This could not go on.

"Attention!" I cried, and the campers looked at me, startled. "I'm in charge here, and I have some orders for the rest of the evening." (Freddie and Donna groaned.) "You *must* stay up past midnight!" I announced. (A few smiles appeared.)

"You *must* get all that junk food out and *eat it*!" (A giggle.) "Most important, I order you to scare each other to death with ghost stories!"

Everyone began to laugh. They rushed for the junk food. Then they gathered on a couple of the bunks. I think the girls were relieved to know that it was okay to have fun even though Charlene was going through a bad time.

I glanced at Amy and we smiled at each other.

Then I glanced at Heather's bunk and saw her there, curled up with *The Grey King*, looking solitary.

I sighed.

CHAPTER 14

Monday

Dear Henry and Grace,

HI, you two! How is New
York? I miss you and it a lot.
Have you had any other baby-
sitters while I've been gone?
I can't wait to come back and
take you to the Central Park
Zoo, or maybe to the Last
Wound-Up to look at toys one
afternoon while your parents
are working.
Camp is fine.

Love,
Stacey

Henry and Grace Walker

14 West 81st Street, Apt. 18E

New York, NY 10023

Camp is not fine at all. I am in the infirmary. That's *the infirmary*. Why did Dawn have to show *The Parent Trap* to everyone so many times? (Actually, I'm exaggerating a little. Things aren't bad here.)

How did I end up in the infirmary? Good question. Well, I was just fine when I got to Camp Moosehead last week. And it isn't my diabetes that's the problem, thank goodness. That's entirely under control. This all started a couple of days ago when I began noticing funny things. First of all, I just plain didn't feel well. Kind of achy and tired. I thought maybe I really *was* just tired, that I wasn't used to all this exercise and running after six-year-olds twenty-four hours a day. Then I started itching. No matter what I was doing, I would find a new itchy spot somewhere on my body.

I was taking Karen Brewer and Nonie to the bathrooms one day when I glanced in the mirror and found a scaly, itchy spot near my mouth.

"What'sh that?" asked Nonie.

"The plague," I replied. I was not in a good mood. I had already found a large red itchy bump on my shoulder that day.

The next day I was helping Monique to make a bracelet in arts and crafts, when she looked at me with alarm. "What's that?" she asked.

I was about to reply, "The plague," again, since I was tired of the question, when I looked where she was pointing. Spreading down my arm, away from the red bump on my shoulder, was a rash. I scratched it experimentally. It was the itchiest of all my itchy things.

Suddenly, I felt chilled. Not the kind of chill you feel when you're sick (that was *one* symptom I didn't have), but the kind of chill you get when you realize something horrible. I was remembering Mrs. Means's announcements on the first night of camp. I was remembering what she'd said about Lyme disease. Flu-like symptoms (I was achy and tired, wasn't I?) and the spreading rash. Well, that bump on my shoulder had spread pretty far.

"Can I go back to the cabin?" I asked the arts and crafts counselor. "I don't feel too good."

"Sure, go ahead, Stacey," she replied, worried. "Nonie, go with her. See that she's okay."

Nonie. Of all campers. But I was much too weak to argue.

Nonie led me back to 6-B. She stayed ten feet away from me and wouldn't touch me. "I'm sure you're 'tagioush," she said sweetly. "Have you had the chicken pocksh? That thing by your mouth looksh like the chicken pocksh."

Well, I *had* had the chicken pocksh, I mean pox, but I'd heard it was possible to get the disease twice.

The chicken pox? I had Lyme disease *and* the chicken pox?

"And your eyesh look awfully red," Nonie added helpfully as she watched me lie down on my bunk.

Well, maybe red eyes was one of the flu-like symptoms of Lyme disease. More likely, I had developed allergies, possibly to my clothes and sleeping bag.

"Shtashey?" Nonie spoke up tentatively.

"You can go back to arts and crafts now," I told her. "I'll be all right." (I was practically dead.)

"But your rash. It'sh short of all over. Look at your armsh and legsh."

I looked. The rash *was* all over and I itched all over.

I sneezed. Darn old allergies. And I realized my stomach didn't feel so great. Probably dyspepsia.

"You know what, Nonie?" I said, struggling to my feet. "I think I better get to the infirmary."

"Do you want me to go with you?" Nonie asked, backing away.

"No, that's okay."

"Oh, thanksh." Nonie hightailed it out of the cabin. She was probably heading for the bathrooms so she could take a shower and wash off any of my germs that might have hopped onto her.

I walked to the infirmary, feeling extremely sorry for myself. I stepped inside.

The nurse took one look at me and nearly fainted. I must have been sicker than I thought. Leprosy, maybe.

Just in case, I turned around. Nope, no one was behind me. It really was me the nurse was fainting over.

"I have Lyme disease," I told her dispiritedly, as if I barely cared anymore. "And allergies and dyspepsia and the chicken pocksh. I mean, pox."

The nurse recovered. "You don't look so hot, that's for sure. Come on and lie down. I'm Miss Dinsmoore. And you're lucky because the camp doctor visits today. He'll be able to prescribe a course of treatment. For now we better put something on that poison ivy."

"Poison ivy?" I repeated.

"It's all over you."

"This rash? On my arms and legs?"

"Yup. It's the worst case I've seen in years. What did you do? Roll around in the leaves? You do know what poison ivy looks like, don't you?"

I didn't, but I remembered the nice patch of leaves I'd found to sit in on that first night at camp. And come to think of it, I'd been itchy ever since then. It was just that the rash had been spreading and thickening lately.

I'll spare you guys the really gross details of the doctor's visit, and just tell you that my "Lyme disease" was actually a big mosquito bite surrounded by poison ivy, my red eyes were allergies, my sneezing and aches and tiredness were a cold, the disgusting thing by my mouth was impetigo, and all the itchiness was from more insect bites and, of course, the poison ivy. (The dyspepsia was a nervous stomach, which cleared up as soon as I found out I didn't have Lyme disease.)

"Well," said Miss Dinsmoore, after the doctor had left, "I know you are one uncomfortable young lady."

I nodded miserably. Maybe they would send me home.

"So you'll be staying here for a few days."

"Here? In the infirmary?"

Miss Dinsmoore nodded. "You'll need a few things."

Karen Brewer was given the job of bringing over my nightgown, toothbrush, injection kit, and the Stephen King book I was now reading.

You might think this was the low point of my Camp Moosehead stay. It wasn't. Getting sick and going to the infirmary was the worst part. Now was the beginning of the best part. First of all, I got a roommate. I'd been the only patient in the infirmary until Miko Tyrrell arrived. Miko was a CIT with a broken leg and a cast up to her thigh. She had been in the emergency room of the hospital in the nearest town. (She broke her leg when she fell off a horse.)

I could see that Miko was in much worse shape than I was, but even so she kept smiling and laughing. And she had lots of visitors. So did I, thanks to my friends and my campers. Soon the infirmary was like a party. Twice, Miss Dinsmoore had to ask us to keep it down, although I don't know why, since no one was sleeping. (But Miss Dinsmoore kept taking aspirins.)

Now it is Monday and I'm going to be allowed to leave the infirmary soon. My puffy eyes and impetigo are pretty much healed. My cold has cleared up. And although I'm still covered with Calamine lotion, my bites and poison ivy feel a *lot* better.

"I wish you could leave soon, too," I said to Miko.

Miko smiled. "Well, at least I get my crutches tomorrow. And I *am* at camp for the rest of the summer. Things could be worse."

She was right. They could be. I knew it the instant Nonie walked in. Now that I wasn't contagious, she wasn't afraid to come near me. Practical-joke worries poured into my head. I remembered peppery chewing gum and a few other things.

But Nonie just sat at the edge of my bed and chatted with Miko and me.

"I'll be helping you back to our cabin tomorrow," she informed me. "I'll carry your things for you."

"Great," I replied, smiling. Maybe camp was okay after all.

Nonie left then. But as she stepped outside and passed the window by my bed, she shot a rubber band in at me. Then she ran away, giggling.

Guess what? I laughed, too.

CHAPTER 15

Monday

Dear Bart,

Well, here I am at camp. It isn't exactly what I expected, but it's, well, an adventure. I guess that's what camp should be, right? How are the Bashers doing? Are you getting them together for team practices, or are your kids all off at camp, too? My kids are getting plenty of softball practice right here (some of them are, anyway), so I'm not too worried about them. In fact, my Krushers challenge your Bashers to a game when we're back in Stoneybrook. And how about if you and I rent a movie? I'll watch anything except _Meatballs_!

    — Kristy,
     Krushers' coach

Bart Taylor
65 Edgerstoune Drive
Stoneybrook, CT 06800

Two things my stepfather is always saying (and there are a lot of things Watson is always saying) are: one, that life is full of ups and downs, and two, that you have to take the good with the bad. Since camp is part of life, I guess it follows that camp would be full of ups and downs, and also that you'd have to take the good with the bad here.

That does seem to be true. Take Charlotte Johanssen. She is an up and a down just by herself. And so are my days here. Some are ups. Some are downs. They all have goods and bads.

After that first awful night here, when Charlotte cried and cried and called home, and after letting us know all the things about camp that she's afraid of (horses, the lake, etc.) she's still here. Something is keeping her. (I sure wish I could talk to Stacey about her, but I don't want to worry Stacey while she's in the infirmary. She's got enough on her mind without having to wonder about Charlotte.)

One day Charlotte cried because she didn't want to be in a volleyball game against another cabin. (The ball scared her.) Another time she cried because a counselor yelled at a kid. (This had nothing to do with Charlotte.) A third time, she cried during a nature movie when a close-up shot of a bullfrog puffing out his throat frightened her.

Each time, I took Char someplace private and quiet, knelt to her level, took her hands, and said, "You know you can go home, don't you? Becca and I would be so happy if you stayed here, but if you want to go home, you really, really can. It wouldn't be the first time a camper went home early."

And each time, Charlotte sniffled, wiped her eyes, and said she wanted to stay.

"Are you sure?" I asked.

"Positive."

Charlotte did like arts and crafts. And she did like the nature cabin (except for the bullfrog movie), and she had very much enjoyed a scavenger hunt. She was also nervous but excited about the dance that Mallory and Jessi were teaching my campers. But were those things worth all the tears and fears in between? I wasn't sure. There must have been something else keeping Charlotte at Camp Moosehead. (But I didn't know what it was, and wouldn't find out until later.)

Me? Well, here's a list of the good things I took with the bad:

— sailing
— water-skiing
— swimming
— softball
— watching my kids rehearse for Parents' Day

Here's a list of the bad things I took with the good:

— arts and crafts
— the nature cabin
— living with so many people breathing down my neck
— constantly being mentally made over by the other CITs
— being talked into going to that dance on Wednesday (I had figured out a way to skip it.)
— *actually* being made over by the CITs before the dance (This hasn't happened yet.)

I guess I better explain some of these things, since they probably don't make a lot of sense. I think the top list is self-explanatory, except for the last thing. I love sports, so of course I'm in seventh heaven at Camp Moosehead. I even got my swimming badge. But the Parents' Day program ... My kids are having the best time rehearsing their routine!

I can't believe it. Even Charlotte, with her homesickness and stage fright, seems to be enjoying herself more. This is for several reasons. For one thing, she's found out that she won't have to perform alone — she's in on a special project with

Becca and her other fellow campers. Also, Jessi and Mallory are giving the girls tons of encouragement and attention. I'm sure the campers think they'll go right from Camp Moosehead to the stage at Lincoln Center in New York City. And Jessi and Mal have worked out a sort of dance-and-skit routine (a musical, I guess) that is fun, funny, and touching.

But the girls' rehearsals are a riot. At first they insisted on wearing tight socks on their feet so that they looked like they were dancing in ballet shoes. But the socks on the wooden floor were so slippery that everyone kept falling down and Jessi finally had to get mats for the girls to dance on.

Even with the mats, there are spills. Once, Becca (who, I'm sorry, but she doesn't have much of Jessi's talent) reached a crucial point in the routine. She was supposed to make a leap across the mats to Charlotte and two other girls, who would catch her and slowly lower her face down until she was lying on her stomach. She had done this once before and it was very dramatic-looking. But this time she leaped, arced through the air, and landed on her right foot, which just skidded forward and knocked over Charlotte and a few others. The girls laughed so hard that one of them wet her pants, which caused everyone else to laugh even harder, which caused Becca to wet *her* pants.

Jessi and Mal called an end to the rehearsal. Even they were laughing.

Meanwhile, some of the bad things that I took with the good were underway. I'm sure I don't have to explain my feelings about arts and crafts and the nature cabin. Those are just not for me. (Or in Watson's words, they're not up my alley.) But the rest of it . . .

It had started on the first day of camp. I could feel the eyes of the other CITs — Tansy, from my cabin, and Lauren and Izzy from 8-A — on me at all times. They weren't even subtle about it. They made those outright comments about needing blush and letting my bangs grow out. In between, they just stared, their eyes calculating. I could see them thinking: pluck her eyebrows, cover up that pimple, perhaps get a nose job. Why didn't they just trade me in for a new CIT, one with fashion sense?

I began to worry about the upcoming CIT dance. No way was I going to it. Not if it meant being scrutinized by Tansy, Izzy, and Lauren. Plus, what if they tried to set me up with someone?

I could see only one way out.

Poison ivy.

I would roll around in Stacey's leafy patch, and by the night of the dance I'd be a disgusting, itchy mess. I'd be a prisoner in the infirmary.

This was before the CITs' free hour earlier today. As soon as the campers went off with the counselors, I found myself surrounded by Tansy, Lauren, and Izzy. They sat me in a chair and attacked me — not with fists or words, but with eyebrow pencils, blush, eye shadow, tweezers, mascara, hair goo, scissors, and some things I don't have names for.

They didn't exactly make me over, but they experimented. And all the time they experimented, they shined a bright light in my face, making the torture effect more real. I kept my eyes closed during the ordeal. Finally it was over.

"Open your eyes," said Lauren.

Reluctantly, I did so.

Izzy was holding a mirror in front of me. Some stranger's face was in it.

"Angle it differently," I said. "I can't see myself."

Tansy giggled. "That's *you*, Kristy."

I have to admit that I did not look revolting. I certainly looked better than if I'd been covered with poison ivy. And I certainly felt better than if I'd been covered with poison ivy. But I had a feeling this meant I would have to go to the dance.

"This isn't everyday wear, is it?" I asked hopefully.

"*No,*" said Izzy, smiling. "It's dance wear and you know it."

I nodded.

"You are going to have a terrific time at the dance," said Tansy.

Maybe, maybe not. Easy for them to say.

The face in the mirror was attractive, pretty, even glamorous. But it wasn't the face of Kristin Amanda Thomas. It was the face of someone who should feel much older, and I didn't feel older. I didn't feel grown-up. I didn't even feel like an in-charge Baby-sitters Club president. If I had to go to the dance as a false Kristy, I would be embarrassed. I would be a bomb.

And I did not like this group arrangement, this cabin full of people, with everyone living my life for me. I needed space. I needed privacy. I needed separateness.

Charlotte did, too.

Why on earth was she still at Camp Moosehead?

CHAPTER 16

Tuesday

Hi, Janine!

How are you. Camp is fine.
I'm looking for a boyfreind.
I know that sonds funny
but waht I mean is I'm looking
for this ~~post part~~ certin
boy I saw and I know he likes
me and I like him but we
don't no each others names.
This is a real ~~do doti~~ problem.
I'll will find him though,
don't you worry and I'll give
you a reprot when I see you.

Love your sister,
Claudia

Janine Kishi

58 Bradford

Stoneybrook, Connec 06800

Right after lunch on Tuesday, I could tell that something was up with my campers. Nine-year-olds are not particularly good at keeping secrets, and my group was no exception, especially when it came to R-O-M-A-N-C-E. And *especially* when they'd gotten to play the role of matchmakers (sort of).

When lunch was over, Meghan and the other counselors took their break, and it was the job of the CITs to return to the cabins with their campers for a rest hour, during which everyone is supposed to write letters or postcards home. Now Sally, my co-CIT, and I have noticed some dedicated letter-writers among our campers, particularly Vanessa Pike and Gail, the quiet campers. But that day, even they just dashed off sloppy cards and threw down their pens. The campers kept exchanging glances and hiding giggles.

"Okay, what's going on?" I asked from my perch on top of Sally's and my bunk.

Nobody tried to hide a thing. The campers all began talking at once.

"We *found* him!" exclaimed Haley.

"Him? Him who?" I asked.

"Him *who*? Your cute guy, that's who. The boy of your dreams," said little Jayme.

I nearly fainted. "You — you did? How? You mean you know his name?"

"Don't worry about how we did it," said Leeann. "This summer is the fourth one Jayme and I have spent at Camp Moosehead. We know everything — including how to get in touch with the boys' side."

I didn't ask any questions. I had a feeling I was better off not knowing what they knew.

"Your cute guy," said Jayme importantly, "is named Will Yamakawa. And he'll definitely be at Movie Night tonight."

I couldn't believe it! They'd found my mystery boy. I hadn't been able to see him before Movie Night, like I'd wanted, but . . . they knew his name. They knew where and when I could meet him. Furthermore, he was Japanese, like me, which would please my parents a great deal. They've never said so, but I'm sure they want me to carry on our family heritage by marrying a Japanese man and having Japanese children. Not that Will and I had plans for that sort of thing yet (he didn't even know me), but Mom and Dad would certainly be pleased to hear about him. My other crushes — Trevor Sandbourne and Austin Bentley — had not been Japanese, and I always knew that disappointed my parents. Boy, what a way to please them — finding the world's cutest (Japanese) boy.

"Gosh!" I exclaimed. "How can I ever thank

you guys? I can't believe what you did." (I hoped nobody would be in any trouble.)

"You can thank us," Haley replied, looking sly, "by giving us a report on the evening. A *full* report," she added.

"I'll do my best," I told the girls.

The CIT movie program was to start at seven-thirty that night. As soon as dinner (if you could call it that) was over, my campers and Sally and I raced back to our cabin, where I dressed in my best moose clothes and then went to the bathrooms and put on makeup and jewelry and tied a ribbon in my hair. I didn't want to go all out, though. The dance was the next night, and with any luck I would see Will again. And I would want to look extra-extra-special then.

"Wish me luck!" I called to Vanessa, Haley, and the others, as Sally and I boarded the Camp Moosehead mini-van that would drive us around the lake. As we were looking for seats, I wanted to tell Mary Anne that taking the van around the lake was a lot easier than taking a midnight hike, but she wasn't on the van. Neither was Dawn. I had heard a rumor about some kind of camp crisis, but no one else knew much about it or seemed too concerned, so the van pulled away. I was surprised that Mary Anne was passing up a chance to see Logan, though.

Bump, bump, bump. After the world's most jolting ride (not a great idea following a Camp Moosehead dinner) we arrived at the other side of the lake. The boy CITs were waiting to greet us.

It was Tuesday evening. Camp would be over in four days. There was not a second to lose. I jumped off the bus, spotted Will in the crowd, elbowed my way over to him, and said, "Hi, I'm Claudia Kishi. I met you last week when you came to tell us about the movie and the dance."

Will's face broke into a smile. "Claudia," he said. "So that's your name. I was, um, too nervous to ask. How did you know I wanted to meet you? And how did you find out who I am? John didn't introduce Jeremy and me, did he?"

I shook my head. "My campers did a little research," was all I replied.

Will and I were just standing there grinning at each other. Ah, love at first sight, I thought. At last I *truly* knew the meaning of it.

Will walked me into the recreation hall, where the movie was to be played. "Some of my friends tried to get a scary movie," he told me conspiratorially, "but it didn't work out. We're going to see *Meatballs*, with Bill Murray."

"*Meatballs*?!" I squeaked. "They're showing us a *camp* movie at *camp*?"

Will nodded and made a face.

We sat in the back, where we could talk and not pay attention.

I guess we talked a little too much.

"Shh!" said someone.

"SHH!" said someone else a moment later.

"*SHHHHHHH!*" said about eight people not long after that.

"Want to go outside?" asked Will.

I nodded. I was afraid to say any words. I might have been attacked by the audience.

Will and I tiptoed out of the rec hall. We sat on the concrete steps to the doorway.

"Is this your first summer at Camp Moosehead?" asked Will.

"Yup. Yours?"

"Nope. Third."

"Where are you from?"

"Ashfield, New York. You?"

"Stoneybrook, Connecticut."

After we got the boring facts straight, we began discussing more serious things. I forget how we got onto the subject, but Will told me that his grandmother had always lived with his family.

"Mine, too!" I exclaimed. "We are *so close*, my grandmother and I. I can tell her anything and know she'll understand. My family calls her Mimi. What do you call your grandmother?"

"Well . . . well, um, we called her Tink. It's a long story. But she died last month. She'd been really sick."

"Oh. I'm sorry." At first I didn't know what else to say. Then I said, "I guess this is a dumb question, but do you miss her?"

"All the time. It's weird. I go around doing whatever I have to do — helping my campers, eating, sleeping, laughing, brushing my teeth. But it's like there's this hole inside me and I'm always aware of it and it never fills up."

"Do you cry?" I whispered.

"Sometimes."

Just then, the doors burst open and the CITs poured out of the rec hall. The movie was over. Will and I were almost trampled. But we struggled to our feet and followed the others to a campfire, where we were going to roast marshmallows (mmm, junk food) before us girls had to go back to the other side of the lake.

Will found a stick for us and put four marshmallows on it. He toasted them until the outsides were almost black and the insides were oozing out. Then he pulled the first two off and gave them to me while he ate the others. We licked our fingers and stared at the fire.

Stacey and Kristy were there, but I didn't see them. I wasn't aware of anything except the crackling fire and the moonlight and Will sitting next to me. After a long time, he reached over and took my hand. A chill went down my back. He didn't let go until the CIT van pulled up and I reluctantly had to leave him.

CHAPTER 17

Wednesday

Dear Granny and Pop-Pop,

As my friend Claudia would say, "Oh, my lord!" You absolutely will not believe what happened when my campers and I went out on our overnight. Parts of it were the scariest times of my life, parts were fun, parts of it were exciting. Most of it was unexpected. What happened? I think I better wait to tell you. But really and truly we are all safe and wound. Boy, I bet I've got you curious now. Oh well, I'll probably see you before you get this postcard.

I love you and miss you,
Dawn

Granny and Pop-Pop Porter

747 Bertrand Drive

Stoneybrook, CT

06800

The day after Charlene left, Debra arrived. She was going to be our new counselor. She had been a CIT at Camp Moosehead last summer. That was it. One year of being a CIT. She's only two years older than I am. But she seemed nice. And she didn't mind that her very first activity was to take Amy, me, and six eleven-year-olds on an overnight camping trip.

"I went last summer," she said. "I remember it well."

We were all packed (we had been for days) so we were ready to go. A backpack and sleeping bag were strapped to each of us, and we planned to take turns carrying the rest of our equipment and provisions — tents, food, cooking stuff, first aid kit, etc.

We set out right after lunch on Monday.

We'd walked all of two steps when Heather said, "You've got the compass, haven't you, Debra?"

Debra's eyes opened wide. "Oops," she said. She ran back to the cabin to retrieve it.

"Good going," I said gratefully to Heather, and the first twinge of worry darkened my good mood.

"And someone's got the extra canteens, just in case, don't they?" said Heather.

"Extra canteens?" I repeated. I chased Debra back to the cabin.

At last we were truly on our way. Debra took the lead, followed by three campers, then Amy, three more campers, and then me, bringing up the rear. Heather was right in front of me. For some reason, I felt relieved.

We'd had an exciting send-off back at camp, with Mrs. Means yelling at us to have fun and be careful (she must know Stacey's mother), but now we were on our own. The woods seemed awfully quiet. I tried to think of them simply as peaceful, though. After all, I am a nature girl and should feel at home in the woods.

The route we were to follow was marked by cairns. Every overnight trip follows the same route to the same campsite in the woods. The campsite is about five miles from the center of Moosehead — a pretty good hike. There are paths throughout the woods near camp, because the younger campers take nature walks and go on short day hikes and that sort of thing. But since Moosehead is in a fairly remote area of the state, it's possible to walk dozens of miles from Old Meanie's and still be in the wilderness. (This according to Heather, who was speaking up and sounding quite knowledgeable.)

Anyway, the route for the overnight is marked by those cairns. Cairns are piles of stones that used to be used as memorials (I think), but can also be used as sort of traffic signs in the woods. They tell you which direction to follow to get where you want to go. Let's say you reach an intersection of two paths and you find a stack of stones piled on the ground near the intersection with one stone set to the right of the stack. That cairn would tell you to turn right. If the stone were set to the left of the stack, you would turn left. If you saw simply a stack of stones, that would mean to go straight ahead. Sometimes we would find a straight-ahead cairn where there was no intersection. That was just to let us know we were still on the right track. (I found those cairns pretty reassuring.)

Our campers loved watching for the cairns and following their directions. Rachel's bionic vision allowed her to spot a cairn before anyone else, and then yell out where we were going.

"Let's sing," said Caryn after awhile. "Let's sing, like, an old rock and roll song from the fifties. Something with a good beat that we can march to."

"I've got a song," announced Shari. " 'Monster Mash.' Do you guys know that one?"

We weren't sure.

"Well, I'll start singing it. You'll recognize it after awhile, I'm sure. They play it on the radio all the time around Halloween. Okay. Here goes. I think I have the words right. *I was working in my lab late one night —*"

(And suddenly we remembered the song.)

"*He did the Mash!*" we sang, giggling. "*He did the Monster Mash.*" Some of us weren't too sure of the words at this point when Heather, who *hadn't* been singing, cried out, "Uh-oh!"

Her "Uh-oh!" was loud enough to stop the rest of us in our tracks (and in our song).

"What-oh?" said Freddie.

Heather pointed to a cairn we were about to miss because we were so involved in our song. The cairn was at an intersection, but it had fallen down. It was just a pile of stones.

"Which way do we turn?" asked Amy nervously.

"Don't worry. I've got a map of the woods," said Debra, pulling it out. She studied it for a moment. Our marching line fell apart as Amy and the campers and I gathered around Debra and the map. I don't know why I even looked at it. I may be good at math, but I can't read maps too well. I can barely tell my left from my right, let alone north from south or east from west. The map just looked like a lot of squiggly lines. And where were *we* on the map, anyway?

"Okay," said Debra, folding up the map and sticking it under her belt. "We turn left here."

"I don't think so," said Heather. "I think we turn right." But Debra didn't hear her.

We turned left. We walked and walked and marched and marched and sang and sang. By six o'clock we hadn't seen another cairn, but thanks to Debra and her map, we'd made all sorts of turns and would never be able to trace our steps back to that last broken cairn (as if that would have helped).

Debra came to a standstill and so did the rest of us. "Um," she said, "um, I think we're — we're lost. Don't panic, anybody, but I do think we're lost."

I don't know how everyone else felt, but I was ready to panic when Heather said, "I see a clearing." She pointed ahead of us. "Why don't we just make camp there? We have to stop soon anyway to eat and sleep. We can't go tramping through the woods all night."

Everyone was amazed. Until this trip, no one had heard Heather say much more than two sentences at a time. And since her suggestions were reasonable and we were pretty tired, we did exactly as she said. We walked to the clearing and unloaded our gear. Shari, the clown, made a great show of trying to unfasten her pack and toppling over backward, claiming she was off-balance. "I can't get up!" she cried, like a turned-over tortoise.

We began to make camp. We set up the tents. (One collapsed on Freddie.) We unrolled our sleeping bags. We built a fire — finally. We couldn't get it going until Heather stepped in to help us. We stared at her, surprised and grateful. (Nobody had said a mean thing to her since she'd found our campsite.)

"Okay, dinner," announced Debra. You could tell she was trying to be cheerful but was scared to death.

"Dinner?" said Shari. "Don't you mean chow?"

"Whatever."

"I think," spoke up Donna, and I could tell some great plan was about to come pouring out of her mouth, "that we better save our rations," (rations?) "and live off the land for awhile. Just in case we aren't rescued soon. I'll go try to catch a rabbit or something. You know, you can even eat rattlesnake meat. It's considered a real delicacy."

"*You* eat it," said Rachel, at the same time Caryn squeaked, "You're going to catch a *rattlesnake*?" and Freddie said, "And just who is going to skin the rabbit?"

I don't think I need to tell you that what we ate

for dinner was just what we had packed — hot dogs and beans, which we cooked over the fire; water from our canteens; and later, marshmallows. (I skipped the marshmallows but I did manage to choke down a hot dog. It was either that or starve. The hot dog was okay as long as I didn't think about what was in it.)

We sat around the campfire with our marshmallows (actually, some people made s'mores) and told ghost stories. We were more scared than usual, which didn't surprise me, considering we were lost.

And then Rachel, darn her, said, "You know, I heard that some murderers escaped from that prison in Peacham."

A hush fell over the group around the campfire.

"And since we don't know where we are," Rachel continued, "maybe we're right near Peacham. Maybe we're near them. Maybe —"

"Aughh!" (That was sort of a group scream.)

Everyone gobbled their marshmallows and s'mores, put out the fire, and dove for the safety of the tents, although the tents couldn't keep out mosquitoes, let alone murderers.

No one slept much that night and we were all quite tired the next morning, but surprised to find ourselves alive. Furthermore, we were so scared that we decided to eat a very fast breakfast and then just head back to Camp Moosehead, wherever that was. While Debra studied the map, with Heather looking over her shoulder, the rest of us scarfed down some granola bars and then began to break camp. We packed up in record time.

We set off again in the direction Debra was sure would lead us back to Camp Moosehead. We walked for three hours.

"My backpack is killing me," announced Freddie.

Heather showed her how to adjust it.

"I'm starving," said Amy.

"We better watch our food supply," said Heather.

I realized that the campers seemed somewhat comforted by Heather, and were definitely glad to have her around. Everyone except Debra was going to her with their problems.

"How do you know all this stuff?" I finally asked Heather.

"One of the books I read last week was a camping and survival manual."

I couldn't help smiling at Heather and she actually grinned back at me. I could tell she was proud of herself — and I was proud of her for being proud of herself!

By five o'clock that afternoon we should have

been back at Camp Moosehead. But we were nowhere near it. Or maybe we were, since we didn't know where we were.

"Hey!" cried Amy. "Isn't that where we spent last night?"

We ran to a nearby clearing. There were the remains of our dampened campfire. There were the holes where we had pitched our tents.

"Now what?" The question came from Debra, who didn't look nearly so sure of herself anymore.

"May I please have the map?" asked Heather.

Debra handed it over.

"I know where we are," said Heather. "I know where we need to go. I think we should stay here tonight because it's a long walk back to camp. Then would you please let me lead the way home tomorrow?"

"Yes!" cried everyone.

We set out very early the next morning, knowing Mrs. Means and the rest of the camp were worried to death. We figured 11-B hadn't even been allowed on their overnight and we felt bad about that. But we struggled along, following Heather's directions.

After two hours, we heard voices. Then shouts.

"There they are! There they are!" It was a

search party from camp. I saw Stacey and Mary Anne and just about everyone.

Our group ran to the search party. Mary Anne and I hugged and cried. "I knew something was wrong last night," she said, "but no one would say what it was. I didn't even go to Movie Night. Oh, I am *so* glad to see you. And guess what. You're back in time for the CIT dance!"

I couldn't help laughing. A minute ago I'd been lost in the woods, and now we were talking about dances.

Our rescuers led us back to camp. When we reached it, Mrs. Means gave Heather a Camp Moosehead bravery medal.

We all deserved one, I thought, but Heather deserved it the most.

Wednesday

Dear Mimi,

Guess what happened today, but please, please don't tell my father, if you see him. He would kill me, even though it wasn't my fault. The other CITs in my cabin and the cabin next door dared me to let them pierce my ears. Even though we get along okay now, I'm tired of them still sometimes trying to prove that I'm not really a cool person. So I said they could just go ahead and do it if it was so important to them. Did they do it or not? I'll show you when I get home!

Love and hugs,
Mary Anne

Mrs. L. Yamamoto

58 Bradford Court

Stoneybrook, CT

06800

I absolutely cannot believe it. Randi, Faye, and Julie wanted to *pierce* my *ears*. Well, they did, and here's the story: Ever since I tried to sneak around the lake, they've treated me with a lot more respect. But sometimes — just sometimes — I get the feeling that they're still testing me a little. Once, Tara asked me for beauty tips for her sister. She said Faye was too shy to ask me. I told the Terror to tell Faye to put avocado mash on her face in order to improve blood circulation, which in turn would give Faye's cheeks such a glow that she'd never need to use blush again. Luckily for all of us, Faye is allergic to avocados so she couldn't try this. I had just made up the theory and was pretty sure the treatment wouldn't do a thing.

As the CIT dance approached, the girls started asking me questions like, Should I wear this blue ribbon in my hair, or this green one? What kind of perfume should I put on to attract a boy without overwhelming him?

I made up answers to the questions. I hoped they were the ones the girls wanted to hear. I hoped they were right.

Then the CITs' Wednesday time-off rolled around. Randi, Faye, Julie, and I were sitting around in 7-B when Faye suddenly said, "Hey, Mary Anne, why don't I pierce your ears?"

Well, now, this was an extremely poor idea. For one thing, long ago my father put his foot down — NO PIERCED EARS. A hard and fast rule. For another thing, I'm not even sure I want holes punched through my earlobes.

But Stacey and Claud and Dawn and Jessi and Mal all have pierced ears and they do look pretty terrific. So, with all that in mind, I said, "Well, I don't know."

"You aren't scared, are you?" asked Faye tauntingly.

"No, of course not."

"Then let me pierce them for you."

I sighed. "All right. If it's that important to you, go ahead. Pierce my ears."

I knew Dad would kill me, and I was afraid of having a nonprofessional job (I did not want to wind up with a raging infection, sharing the infirmary with Miko), but I said yes anyway.

"Yes?" repeated Faye. She looked slightly alarmed.

"Yes," I replied, before I lost my nerve.

"*Yes?*" squeaked Randi and Julie.

"*Yes.*" I was getting impatient.

"Oh. Oh, um, well, let's see what we need here."

There was a long pause. Finally Randi said to Faye, "Come to my bunk. I've got a big needle."

A big needle? Ew, ew, ew! I thought. But I just smiled at Julie as if to say, "I do wild stuff like this everyday."

Julie attempted a smile back at me.

A moment later, the others returned with a needle. A huge needle.

I gulped. But all I said was, "It has to be really, really sharp."

"You've — you've done this before?" asked Randi.

"Just watched a couple of times," I lied. "You've got the thread, don't you? And the nontoxic ball-point pen to mark where you'll make the holes? Oh, and the alcohol?"

I thought that having to track down all those items might put an end to the project, but Faye and Julie went off in search of everything. Randi and I stayed behind. We sat out on the porch, where I pretended to read a book, looking nonchalant, and Randi bit her nails.

I was sure they wouldn't find a nontoxic pen.

A moment later, I heard a triumphant voice cry, "We found everything!"

I dropped my book. "The pen, too?" I asked.

Faye held it out to me. "See? It says 'non-toxic' right here."

"Oh."

We moved back into the cabin. Julie sat me in

a chair. Faye shined a light on me. Randi said, "After they're pierced, we'll put some of my earrings in to keep the holes from closing up. We'll sterilize the earring posts first, of course."

"Of course," I said.

"Why — why don't you come look at my earring box and choose a pair? You need studs with gold posts."

I nodded.

Randi showed me her earring collection. I took much longer than necessary poking through it, and kept purposely holding up earrings that I knew wouldn't be right.

"These?" I asked.

"No, they're hoops," said Randi.

"These?"

"Nope, they have steel posts."

"Oh. These?"

"Those are okay."

Darn it.

"But I was going to wear them to the dance myself," said Randi.

Fantastic!

"Here. Wear these. They're pretty. They're studs. They have gold posts."

Terrific. Just terrific, I thought. But what I said was, "Gosh, thanks, Randi. I can't wait for Logan to see me in them."

"They ought to go nicely with the yellow flower," replied Randi. "And your yellow ribbon."

"Uh, yeah."

"Well," said Faye, "are — are you ready?"

"Sure." I knew darn well that neither one of us wanted to go through with this, but I was *not* going to be the one to back down.

"Okay, sit here," said Faye, pointing to a chair.

I sat. Julie aimed a light at one of my ears and Randi pulled my hair back.

"You're sure you know what you're doing?" I said to Faye.

"Positive. I just numb your earlobe with — Uh-oh. We forgot the ice."

Goody.

But Julie ran to the mess hall and was back with a Baggie full of ice cubes in no time flat.

"Okay," Faye continued. "I numb your ear. Then I stick the threaded needle through it — I think — then I pull the thread out and put the earring in. Or something like that. I'll just play it by ear."

"By *ear*!" cried Randi, and we began to giggle.

We were still giggling when Faye had finished numbing my earlobe and was coming at it with the needle. I closed my eyes and gritted my teeth. But I didn't feel a thing. The ice must really have worked.

I opened my eyes. Faye had drawn back. "I can't go through with this," she said. "I just can't. I've never pierced an ear before, and besides, I can't stand the sight of blood."

We began giggling again. We put the instruments of torture away.

I couldn't wait for Faye and Julie and Randi to meet Logan at the dance. Even though I knew we were good friends, I had to prove to them that he was real — and not a geek or a nerd.

CHAPTER 19

WEDNESDAY

DEAR KERRY AND HUNTER,

HI! HOW ARE YOU? HOW ARE YOUR ALLERGIES, HUNTER? ARE YOU A-CHOOING EVERYWHERE? I HOPE YOU GUYS ARE BEHAVING FOR MOM AND DAD. IF YOU'RE NOT, WATCH OUT. I'LL BE HOME BY THE TIME YOU GET THIS CARD, AND YOU KNOW WHAT I DO TO LITTLE BROTHERS AND SISTERS WHO DON'T LIKE TO BE TICKLED!

TONIGHT THERE'S A DANCE FOR THE CITS. MARY ANNE WILL BE THERE. SO WILL MOST OF THE OTHER GIRLS IN THE BABY-SITTERS CLUB. IT'LL BE A BLAST.

BEHAVE YOURSELVES!

LOVE,

YOUR BIG BROTHER,

LOGAN

KERRY AND HUNTER BRUNO

689 BURNT HILL ROAD

STONEYBROOK, CT 06800

Ever since Mary Anne's letter was delivered to me at lunch the other day, all the guys have made fun of her. They thought her letter was stupid and gooey, and they thought she was a jerk for getting caught sneaking around the lake.

I pointed out that not too many boys had tried to sneak around the lake (so I've heard), and that of those who tried, only two made it. And they were immediately caught on the girls' side by Old Meanie.

Anyway, it was Wednesday night and the recreation hall was ready for the dance. It sure looked different than it had the evening before. The rows of folding chairs from Movie Night were gone. The Meanies had hung red and white crepe paper everywhere and put up bunches of red and white balloons. Hearts were taped to the walls. Unbelievable — the theme of the dance was *Valentine's Day*! Valentine's Day in the middle of summer! Retch. We didn't know this until we peeked into the rec hall after lunch. What a dumb surprise. But you could tell the Meanies were really into it.

I wondered, what with Valentine's Day and all, whether I should try to find a red flower for Mary Anne, but she had asked for a yellow one, so I thought I better follow instructions. And I borrowed some after-shave from my counselor.

Anyway, the afternoon dragged on forever.

Finally supper was over, and the counselors took the campers to an astronomy lecture which us CITs were glad to miss. Instead, we went to our cabins and got ready for the dance. I put on my moose shorts and moose polo shirt and tied my moose sweater casually around my shoulders. Then I put on my cleanest moose socks and my Reeboks. I splashed on the after-shave. I was ready.

"That the flower for the Mary Anne?" asked Rick, pointing to a glass of water next to my bunk. The glass held a perfect yellow daisy. Next to it was a safety pin so I could fasten the flower to Mary Anne's sweater as soon as she stepped off the mini-van.

"No, it's a flower for Old Meanie," I replied, punching him on the arm. "I'm trying to impress her. I want to date her, then run away to the Caribbean with her and live there forever. After a year or so, we won't even remember Mr. Meanie, although he'll spend the rest of his life hiring private detectives to track us down."

Rick laughed. "Just checking," he said.

"Camp bus is here!" shouted Henry from next door. "Let's go, you guys."

Rick, Henry, Cliff, and I hightailed it out of our cabins and reached the flagpole in the middle of camp, just as the van pulled to a stop. We gathered around it eagerly. I hadn't seen Mary Anne since the first day of camp. (I was really disappointed last evening when Kristy had gotten off the bus and said there was some emergency or something and Mary Anne wouldn't be able to come to Movie Night. The CITs were pretty disappointed, too.)

I even began to worry that Mary Anne might not come *tonight*, and then how would I explain things? After that I began to worry that she *would* come. I remembered the first school dance we ever went to together. She was really nervous, but I relaxed her, and when she was finally relaxed enough to dance, her shoe flew off and sailed across the gym, nearly killing someone.

Oh, brother.

But the second I saw Mary Anne step off the bus, I knew everything was going to be okay. I saw Stacey get off, too, (covered with Calamine lotion), and Dawn and Claudia, and finally Kristy, but the only person I greeted was Mary Anne. This was because Mary Anne jumped down the steps of the van, ran to me, and threw her arms around my neck. As soon as she pulled away, I pinned the flower to her sweater. She beamed.

"You got the note," she whispered. "You remembered. I hope you weren't offended, though. I didn't really mean for you to see that note. It was part of something else."

"I figured," I whispered back. "But I didn't mind — much — and I thought you'd like a flower anyway. And look, I put on after-shave."

"You smell nice," said Mary Anne, and we hugged again. When we turned around, we realized we had an audience, a smiling one. I didn't know it until later, but the girl CITs, except for the ones in the Baby-sitters Club, were smiling because they now saw for themselves that I was a real guy, not a bad one at that, and Mary Anne's real boyfriend.

The guy CITs were just grinning to see that so far Mary Anne wasn't a jerk.

The doors to the rec hall were standing open and at either side was one of the Meanies. They ushered us inside. As soon as Mary Anne and I were there, the music began, and kids started to dance. Mary Anne looked at me and said, "I'm getting nervous."

Oh, no. But all I said was, "Well, at least your sneaker can't fly off."

Mary Anne laughed.

"Want to dance?" I asked her.

She nodded.

The first dance was a fast one, which made Mary Anne even more nervous. Slow ones are better because you don't have to dance so much, just sway around. But it was a fast one, and to make things worse, I could feel everyone watching us. I knew why the boys were watching. They wanted to see Mary Anne in action. I guess the girls wanted to see me in action.

We must have passed their tests, though, because after several more dances, Cliff cut in on us. So I cut in on the couple nearest me, and I swear, for the first few seconds of the dance, I didn't even realize I was dancing with Kristy. She looked really different — terrific. Makeup or some other girl thing, I guess. Anyway, wow!

The dance ended and I looked around for Mary Anne, but I couldn't see her, so I switched partners with Henry. As we were switching, he said, "Nice going, Bruno." I knew he was referring to Mary Anne. And the girl I was dancing with, whose name was Randi, believe it or not, said, smiling, "We've heard a lot about you, Logan."

After the next dance, I *still* couldn't find Mary Anne, but I did spot Claudia dancing with this CIT whose name is Will. I cut in on them, but Claudia seemed a little spacey. Actually, very spacey. So spacey that I had to get Will back for her. And at *that* point I finally caught sight of Mary Anne dancing with Rick. I whisked her away and wouldn't let anyone cut in on us for the next three dances.

"I'm getting kind of tired, Logan," Mary Anne said, as the music stopped.

"Let's sit down, then," I said.

A few card tables had been set up near the table with the punch and brownies and stuff on it. We got some plates of food and sat down. Soon Rick, Henry, Cliff, Stacey, Kristy, Dawn, and some other CITs had joined us.

We talked and laughed and made Meanie jokes.

"Where's Claudia?" Stacey asked at one point, but no one had seen her or Will for awhile.

"Nice flower," said Randi to Mary Anne, and she giggled.

"Nice after-shave," said Cliff to me. More laughter.

Not one single person at the tables hadn't heard the story of Mary Anne and the note, but she and her CIT friends told it again anyway, just for fun.

Near the end of the evening, Mary Anne and I crept to a corner of the rec hall, where I gave her a quick kiss. "See you Saturday," I whispered.

"See you Saturday," she replied.

One more kiss.

CHAPTER 20

Thursday

Dear Ashly,

Oh my lord I have met the boy of my draems. Hes name is Will, isn't that a funny name. But he realy is the boy of my draems. There was a dance last nigth and we just danced and daced. Then we talked. And I'll probly never see him agian. Boy is this good matrial for my art. You always say artists need to have expreinces. Well I've had plenty of good ones here. I think maybe my heart is bracking so I will be abel to make a good sclupture or painting from my pain.

See you soon,
Claudia

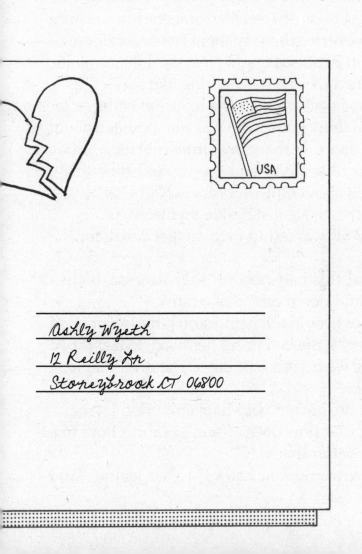

Ashly Wyeth
12 Reilly Ln
Stoneybrook CT 06800

I can't believe it's Thursday. I can't believe the dance is over. I can't believe we go home in two days. I can't believe I might never see Will again. Maybe we'll all have to come back here next summer.

But the dance, oh, the dance. Do I sound like someone in a romance novel? I wouldn't be surprised, because I feel like someone in a romance novel. I never felt this way about Trevor Sandbourne or Austin Bentley. I might have *said* I felt romantic about Trevor, but it was nothing like this.

Let me backtrack a little to last evening, after supper. I don't know who was more excited about the CIT dance — me or my campers. After all, they had sort of set Will and me up and they knew how I felt about him after Movie Night, so by yesterday, they were just beside themselves.

They all wanted to help me get ready for the dance.

"Wear this hair ribbon!" said Vanessa, bouncing up and down on top of a bunk.

Before I could tell her to stop jumping or she'd either break the bed or hit her head, Haley piped up, "No, wear your hair clips. The ones that look like roses."

"No, no, no, put your hair up!" cried Jayme.

"No, let it flow down," said Leeann. "Boys like it much better that way."

"How would you know?" asked Jayme. "You

hair's only two inches long. And you don't have a boyfriend."

"I have a *sister*. An *older* one," said Leeann.

"Okay, okay, girls," interrupted Sally, and I looked gratefully at my co-CIT. "Let Claudia fix her own hair."

"Let me put my makeup on first," I said, heading for the bathrooms. "*Then* I'll decide what to do with my hair."

The campers followed me out of the cabin and into the bathrooms like a line of ducklings. But they did not so much as peep while I fixed myself up. They just pronounced me awesome when I was done.

"Thank you," I said, and once again it was time to board the mini-van and ride around the lake to the boys' side of camp.

This time, every member of the Baby-sitters Club, except for our junior members, were on the van, and we sat together, since we had hardly seen each other since camp began.

No one could get over how fantastic Kristy looked, how tan Dawn had gotten, how pale Mary Anne still was, how poison ivy-covered Stacey was, or how love-struck I was. I couldn't help it. Will was all I could think of. And when the van stopped and the door opened I was one of the first girls off the bus.

He was waiting for me.

I ran directly into his arms. Then we linked elbows and headed into the recreation hall.

It was decorated for . . . "Valentine's Day!" I exclaimed.

"Yeah. Weird, huh?" said Will.

"But kind of nice," I conceded.

"I guess."

"Romantic."

"Yeahhh. . . . Definitely!"

As soon as the music started, Will and I began to dance. Usually, boys want to eat first (eat a *lot*), then dance a little, then rush back to the food, and so forth. But not Will. We danced and danced and danced. I loved the feel of his arms around me, and mine around him.

Soon people began cutting in on each other and switching partners. The first to do that to us was Logan, because someone had cut in on him and Mary Anne. I don't know why, but after maybe half a minute, Logan left me, found Will, and brought him back. I don't remember much about dancing with Logan, but I remember every second of dancing with Will.

Sometimes we danced slowly, talking softly to each other. Sometimes we danced fast and had to yell at each other over the noise of the crowd. Of course, we saved the personal stuff for the slow dances and the funny stuff for the fast ones. Once when we were dancing fast, and the room was *really* noisy, Will yelled, "Mr. Meanie's fly is open!" It wasn't, but it was thrilling to think that you could yell something like that in the person's presence without his knowing it.

Then, in a quiet moment, Will whispered into my ear, "You know what? I feel like Tink is watching me now, and she's happy because she knows I'm happy."

Will's breath on my hair tickled my neck, but all I said was, "That's nice. I hope she's happy for other reasons, too. Do you think that, wherever she is, she's with your grandfather?"

Will looked very serious for a few moments. At last he said, "I don't believe in heaven and hell, but I do believe that the spirits of Tink and Big Papa are together somewhere. So I *know* they're happy. Both of them."

Even though I hadn't known Tink or Big Papa at all, I found that thought comforting.

I was just telling Will that when I felt a tap on my shoulder. I turned around. There was Kristy, smiling bravely. "May I cut in?" she asked.

Oh, my lord. That is something you don't do, no matter what. . . . I don't think. Do you cut in on two people in the middle of a slow dance who look like they're having a heavy conversation?

And do you cut in if you're a girl? I wasn't sure, but I let Kristy have Will for awhile.

Later, we got some food, then stood at the table and talked to our CIT friends for a few minutes. When the music for another slow dance came on, Will looked at me, stood up, and held out his hand. I put my cup of punch down and let him lead me to the dance floor. We swayed from side to side, and I rested my head on Will's shoulder.

Neither of us spoke a word until Will said, "Let's go outside."

So, just like last night, we slipped through the doors. (The Meanies had abandoned their sentry posts.) Then we sat on the steps, held hands, and talked.

I liked the way Will laced his fingers through mine, but I felt sad. "You know, I'll probably never see you again," I said. "Not here at camp after tonight. And you live in Ashfield and I live in Stoneybrook. We're not exactly next door to each other."

"There's always next summer —" Will began.

"Next summer! What about next month, next *week*?"

Will shrugged. He looked awfully serious.

"I don't want us to end," I said, "but I think

we're going to. Even if we are back at camp next summer, a lot can happen in a year."

"I know."

"Maybe we better just say good-bye," I said. And the moment I said that, kids began leaving the rec hall, and the driver of the minivan turned on the motor and headlights. "Oh!" I cried. "I didn't mean right now! I didn't mean we'd have to say good-bye now. . . ."

"I think we do though," said Will in a choked voice.

I began to cry, too. Tears trickled down my cheeks.

We stood up and Will wrapped his arms around me. "I wish I could hold you forever," he said.

"I wish time could stop right now," I added.

And those were the last words we said to each other. We didn't whisper good-bye. We didn't shout out our addresses or phone numbers. Will opened his arms to let me go, and I climbed the bus steps, the last CIT to board. I sat in the back-seat with Stacey and she put her arm around my shoulders, but didn't say anything. I think she knew I wanted to be quiet.

By the time Sally and I reached our cabin, I had stopped crying. We tiptoed inside since the lights were off, and crept to our bunk, but suddenly we were invaded by nine-year-old voices: "How was the dance?" "Did he kiss you, Claudia?" "Did he like you with your hair down?" (That was Leeann, of course.) "What does it feel like when a boy kisses you?" "Jayme, you can't ask her that!"

I was laughing. So was Sally. Thank goodness for our campers. I told them about the evening. (Well, I left out a few parts.) I even told them about not exchanging addresses. They seemed to understand.

We talked and talked, and finally we faded. The next thing I knew, it was Friday morning.

Thursday

Dear Shannon,

Hi! How's Camp Eerie? (I don't think I'd want to be at your camp on Halloween, if camps were open then.) I've been doing tons of sports. Water-skiing is the best. Maybe I'll try skydiving next. Just kidding. That's one thing you can't do here.

If you have seen me last night, I bet you wouldn't have recog nized me. The CIT in my cabin and the ones next door forced me to get dressed up and made up. I didn't look like me at all. I looked like a Kristy Thomas doll. I wonder what Bart would have thought.

Love,
Kristy

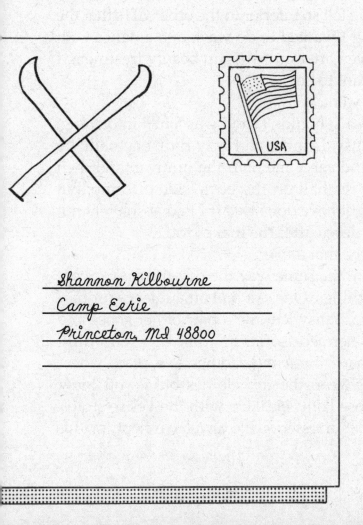

Shannon Kilbourne
Camp Eerie
Princeton, MI 48800

Well, the dance was last night.

I survived.

It must have been a miracle. I think some dance god was watching over me. I don't love dances, but I've gone to some at school. I've even had fun at a few of them. But here at Camp Moosehead — No, let me rephrase that. Here at Cabins 8-A and 8-B I have felt so inferior to the other CITs that the last thing I wanted to do was go to a dance with them. Even after our dry-run beauty treatment, I didn't want to go.

But I went.

I guess I shouldn't say I was *forced* into going, since Tansy, Lauren, and Izzy didn't actually tie me up and carry me onto the minivan and then into the rec hall on the boys' side of camp; but they might have done that if I had absolutely put my foot down after the make-over.

Yes, the make-over.

It went the same way the dry-run had, except for two things. One, we had an audience for part of it. Two, Tansy lent me a pair of her shoes and some of her accessories as well. It's pretty difficult to have the *wrong* clothes at a place where everyone wears the *same* clothes, but as you know, I had those Pony sneakers with the Velcro straps. And . . . *no accessories*. No jewelry except for this bracelet I had to weave in arts and crafts, no ear-rings, head-bands, hair ribbons. Nothing.

So right before dinner, Tansy, Izzy, and Lauren plopped me into a chair and made up my face while our campers were at Open Swim. (Well, Charlotte was just watching Open Swim.)

"But I'm not going to the dance," I said.

"Yes, you are," replied Izzy.

"No, I'm not." (Lauren put something called foundation all over my face.)

"Yes, you are." (Izzy put mascara on my eyelashes.)

"No." (Tansy put on blush. Then she handed me some tan goo and told me to cover up this pimple on my chin. She wouldn't touch it herself, and I don't blame her. But why did *I* cover it up?)

When my face was made up, I looked in the mirror again. Was that really me? Well, of course it was. And I looked pretty. But I still thought the person in the mirror was some remote movie star.

Anyway, after dinner, us CITs had only a half an hour or so before the camp van would take us to the boys' side of the lake. As Tansy, Lauren, Izzy, and I made our final preparations (for take-off?) we drew an audience. Our campers watched us with great interest. They watched as my co-CITs swiftly and expertly put on the proper sneakers and accessories. Then they watched as the CITs sat me in a chair and decorated me like a Christmas tree.

"But I'm not going to the dance," I said.

"Yes, you are," replied Lauren. (She put barrettes in my hair.)

"No, I'm not."

"Yes, you are," said Becca Ramsey. "Tansy, let her try your Reeboks on."

"I'm not going," I repeated.

"No, she isn't," said Charlotte Johanssen. "She's staying here with me." There were tears in Char's eyes and a quaver in her voice.

"Yes. She. Is." That was Izzy. She was putting nonpierced earrings on my ears, taking off my stupid bracelet, and lending me a gold one, plus a necklace.

"Now go into the bathrooms and look at yourself," said Lauren.

All us CITs and campers trooped into the bathrooms, where I stood in front of the mirror. I was penned in, hemmed in. I had no space. I couldn't remember the last time I'd been in a bathroom alone.

"Don't you think you look beautiful?" asked Tansy.

"Yes."

The mini-van pulled up.

"How do you feel?"

"Like I'm going to throw up."

"Good. Stay here with me," said Charlotte.

Becca elbowed Charlotte in the ribs.

"Onto the bus, Kristy," said Izzy, and before I knew it, I was sitting by a window with Mary Anne next to me. Outside, Charlotte was crying loudly.

The bus filled up and pulled away. I did notice that before the campers were out of earshot, Charlotte had stopped crying. I guessed she would be okay until I got back.

Bump, bump, bump. The bus bounced over to the boys' camp. I let everyone get off before me. I watched Mary Anne run into the arms of Logan, and Claudia run into the arms of Will. I considered not getting off the bus, but the driver made me.

Dum, da-dum, dum.

I walked — alone — into a heart-decorated funeral parlor. Well, maybe it wasn't *that* bad.

The first thing that happened was that Tansy appeared at my side and whispered, "When in doubt, hang around the food table. Eating makes you look involved, and when you look involved, you don't stand out so much." She led me through the crowd and over to that table with the punch and brownies and cookies. I realized I was starving, since I'd been too nervous to eat supper, and anyway, who could have eaten vegetable burgers? How could someone even think them up? I bet the Meanies and the cooks didn't eat them.

Tansy and I each took a cup of punch and a brownie. We stood by the table eating until a boy asked Tansy to dance. Then I stood and ate alone until I began to feel ill from brownies. So I approached the dance floor. Lo and behold, a boy asked me to dance! Then Logan cut in on me!! I couldn't believe it!!!

Maybe I was dreaming.

I decided to take the bull by the horns and do something really grown-up. I cut in on Will and Claudia. Will was nice to me, but for some reason, Claudia gave me a dirty look.

Anyway, after awhile, everyone was switching partners and I wound up without one, so I went back to the food table, even though the sight of the brownies made me feel sick. Then I noticed that Stacey, Mary Anne, Logan, Dawn, and a bunch of CITs were sitting around together. Thank goodness. I sat down next to Mary Anne. We talked and laughed. Mary Anne and her co-CITs told the story of Logan and the note. Mary Anne isn't a jerk, but what a thing to do!

I can't say I had a bad time at the CIT dance

that night. I also can't say I wasn't glad to see the mini-van arrive to take us girls back to our cabins. Immediately, I felt more like myself. I was a Kristy-snake shedding my movie star skin so that I could wear my comfortable skin instead. Whew. What a night.

Even though Charlotte had stopped crying by the time I'd left for the dance, I wasn't sure what I'd find when I got back. She survived last evening when I went to Movie Night, but with Charlotte, you never know.

Tansy and I crept into our cabin. Lights off, everyone asleep, even our counselor. To be on the safe side, I tiptoed to Charlotte's bunk and leaned down to look at her.

She woke up immediately. "Hi, Kristy," she mumbled.

"Hi, Char. You doing okay?"

"Mm-hmm. How was the dance?"

"Fine, but I'm glad to be back."

"And I'm glad you are back."

"Thanks. Good night, Charlotte."

"Good night, Kristy."

CHAPTER 22

Thursday

Dear Mom and Dad,

I can't believe you called the infirmary on Monday. I'm not a baby anymore. Sorry. I know that sounds mean. Actually, I was sort of happy you called. But . . . I'M NOT A BABY! Anyway, I'm all well, although my skin doesn't look so hot. The nurse said I won't have scars or anything, though. I'm really glad you let me stay here at camp. I didn't like camp at first, but it's fun now. Guess what—today is Christmas! Confused? You'll probably know all about it by the time you get this card, because two nights from now I'll be back home with you in the Big Apple.

Your itchy daughter,

Stacey

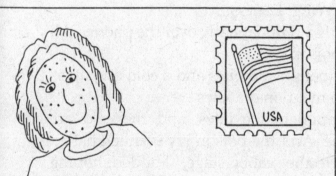

Mr. and Mrs. McGill
14 West 81st Street, Apt. 12E
New York, NY 10023

I could not believe my parents called me in the infirmary on Monday night. I was all set to go back to my cabin the next day. But the camp had had to keep my parents posted on my progress, and by Monday, Mom and Dad thought I'd been in the infirmary long enough and that maybe they should do something about it. Like take me back to New York and put me in a hospital. In the Poison Ivy Wing, I guess.

"Mom," I said impatiently over the phone. "All I've got is poison ivy."

"And impetigo and bites and a cold and allergies. Not to mention diabetes."

"The impetigo, the bites, and the cold are almost gone. And the poison ivy is much better. It's getting to the scabby stage," I added, hoping that if I disgusted my mother she'd change the subject.

"But your diabetes —"

"None of these things are bothering the diabetes. And I'm sticking to my diet and giving myself insulin. The tests have been absolutely normal." (It's sort of gross, I guess, but I have to test my blood everyday. It's simple to do, and the test tells me if there's too much or too little sugar in my blood. I haven't had a problem in months and months, so of course I've been fine here at camp.)

"Well —" Mom began, but before she could finish, Dad got on the extension.

"Hi, honey. Ready to come home?" he asked. "Your mother and I think it's a good idea."

"I don't," I replied.

"Dear?" said Mom.

"Yes?" said both Dad and I.

"I meant your father, honey," Mom told me. "Dear, I don't think she needs to come home after all. Her tests are normal. And she's on the mend."

"My poison ivy is in the scabby stage," I added.

We talked for a few more minutes, and then got off the phone. The last thing my mother said to me was, "Have fun and be careful."

"So?" said Miko from the next bed as I handed the phone back to Miss Dinsmoore.

"I'm staying," I said, and grinned.

Miko grinned back.

The next day, Miko was allowed to get out of bed and try her crutches. She practiced swinging around the room while I packed up my things. I didn't have much to pack and had just about finished when I heard Miko cry, "Whoa-oh! Stacey!"

I spun around in time to see Miko falling. She had caught the tip of one crutch on a chair leg and was pitching forward. I don't know how I got across the room so fast, but I reached Miko in time to catch her and throw her backward onto her bed — which I crashed into. Then I fell to the floor.

"Are you okay?" I asked with a gasp, picking myself up.

"I think so. Gosh, Stacey, you saved my life. I could have been killed."

"Oh, no. Please don't say that. I don't want you following me around, doing me favors for the rest of my life."

We both laughed. Then Miko asked, "Are *you* okay?"

A bump was already coming out on my right knee, and another on my right elbow. And I'd scratched myself on a rough spot on the floor. "Three more wounds," I told Miko. "I don't think anyone will notice."

"Honestly, you two are the Accident Twins," pronounced Miss Dinsmoore, who had come running and had overheard the end of our conversation.

"The Accident Twins," I repeated. "I like that."

The nurse checked us over, decided we really were okay, and said I could still return to my cabin that morning. At eleven o'clock, both Nonie and Karen Brewer showed up to escort me back.

"I'll carry your bag for you," Karen said importantly.

"Thank you," I replied. I was just fine and could easily have carried the bag myself, since I was about to take over my CIT duties again, but Karen wanted very much to be helpful.

"I'm so glad you're coming back, Stacey!" she said, as she and Nonie skipped ahead of me to Cabin 6-B. "You missed some fun stuff, but who knows what might happen next. It could be anything!"

"Are there any other sick people in our cabin now?" I asked warily.

"Nope. Not unless you count the cut on Monique's finger."

I decided not to. I decided to concentrate on staying well. And I did a good job of it, except for getting a splinter in my hand the second I entered 6-B. It was a big splinter and we had to go back to the infirmary so Miss Dinsmoore could take it out.

But after that I stayed accident-free and germ-free for all of Tuesday night, Wednesday, and Wednesday night. I even got to go to the boys' side of camp to see the movie and attend the CIT dance. And during this time, Nonie didn't play one single joke on me. She didn't so much as aim a rubber band at me.

So you can see why I was suspicious on Thursday morning when Nonie woke me up early by bouncing on my bed, crying, "Get up, get up, Shtashey! It'sh Chrishmash!"

"Christmas? Oh, Nonie. Quit kidding. Let me sleep. It isn't time to get up yet."

"But it ish! It ish Chrishmash! *Pleash* look out the window, Shtashey!"

I just knew I was falling for a practical joke, and I hoped that at least I wouldn't get injured. But dragging myself out of bed seemed easier than letting Nonie jump all over me, lisping.

I let Nonie pull me to the window.

Blearily, I looked at the front porch of 6-B. I could not believe my eyes.

It had snowed! Soft, white powder covered the wooden steps and the swing.

Then I turned around and looked *inside* 6-B. How could I have missed what I saw there now? A stuffed stocking hung at the foot of each bunk. A tiny pine tree stood by the doorway. It was decorated with tinsel. A jar of candy canes stood next to it. A wreath was on the door. And —

"Merry Christmas!" Suddenly the campers, the CITs, and the counselor from 6-A burst into our cabin.

The 6-B campers woke up slowly, then became excited and tumbled out of their beds.

"We Christmased you!" cried a 6-A camper.

"Oh, boy!" squealed Monique and Karen and Nonie and the others.

I looked questioningly at Barbara, our counselor.

"During each session of camp," she explained, "One cabin in each age group surprises the other cabin with Christmas in Summer. It's a big secret. No one knows what day will be Christmas."

"Ishn't thish great, Shtashey?" cried Nonie.

"It's merry," I replied.

The 6-B campers were tearing into their stockings, while the 6-A campers looked on, pleased at what they'd accomplished. Inside the stockings were token gifts — candy bars, barrettes, small toys, things the Meanies had provided, I guess.

"Look in your shtocking, Shtashey," said Nonie.

So I did. Someone had taken great care with it. I found sugarless gum, sugar-free hard candy, a pair of moose earrings, a paperback book — and a box of Band-Aids and a bottle of Calamine lotion.

I couldn't help laughing.

Christmas was a wonderful idea. I was liking camp better and better. Too bad I had to go home in two days.

"Nonie," I said, "I've got just one question, and I bet you're the 6-B camper who can answer it. It's at least seventy degrees right now, so what's that snow on our porch?"

Nonie led me to the doorway. We stepped outside. The "snow" rose up in clouds.

"Baby powder," replied Nonie knowingly.

CHAPTER 23

Saturday

Dear Keisha,

Hi, Cousin! This is a silly time to be writing you a postcard, because today is the last day of camp. I'll probably mail this to you from Stoneybrook when I get home tonight. Anyway, camp has been fun (mostly) but today Mallory and I are nervous. As Junior CITs, our job was to teach a dance routine to a group of eight-year-olds for the parents' program today. Boy, has it been a tough job. The girls are not too coordinated. Mal and I want them to do a good job in the show. We also want to prove that we've been responsible, creative Junior CITs. Keep your fingers crossed.

Love, Jessi

Keisha Ramsey
8320 Wagner Lane
Oakley, NJ 07400

So camp was pretty much over. Mal and I had worked hard and played hard and had a good time — even though the other girls in our cabin hadn't exactly warmed up to us, and still called us twins and then laughed, or made other cracks about us.

But on this last morning of camp, Mallory and I weren't thinking too much about those things. There was far too much to do. Everyone had to be packed up so we would be ready when our parents arrived. We had to clean our cabins. And we had to be prepared for the big Parents' Day program. Every single camper had a part in it — either behind the scenes, like Mal and me, or on stage like our dancers.

"On stage" meant in the amphitheater. That was the only place big enough to seat the parents. They would sit around and above the performers, who would be on the ground in the middle of the theater. I guessed that, for this reason, a bunch of programs had been rained out in other years.

Ours wasn't. The sky was blue and cloudless, the sun shining brightly. I began to worry dreadfully.

"What have we gotten ourselves into?" I asked Mal in the bathrooms that morning. "Our dancers are still klutzes. Charlotte hasn't gotten over her stage fright."

"And we don't know how our bunkies, or anyone else, for that matter, are going to react to the musical we wrote," Mal finished up for me.

"Right. They might not get the point. They might think we're just trying to make them feel mean or dumb."

Maybe I better stop here and explain the routine Mal and I wrote for our campers. It's a combination dance/play — a mini-musical. It tells a story through both dance and words. And considering what our bunkies put Mal and me through during these last two weeks, the point we were trying to get across wasn't too subtle. It was about friendship and trust and being Black or white.

The story is of twin girls who move to a new neighborhood. Because they're new and are considered "outsiders," most of the other kids tease them. They taunt them and jeer at them and insult them. The dancing at that point consists of the taunters surrounding the twins and dancing faster and faster, not allowing them to escape. But one of the neighborhood kids hangs back and just watches. She thinks that what the other kids are doing is wrong. So she waits until the mean ones have left, and then she introduces herself to the twins. But the twins don't trust her. (Why should they?) However, through some dialogue, some more dance, and some simple acrobatic moves, the audience sees the twins learn to trust, and a friendship begins.

Nice, simple story, huh? Guess who Mal and I cast as the twins?

Becca and Charlotte.

A Black girl and a white girl.

The campers in 11-B were going to be mortified or angry or both.

"Or maybe ashamed and apologetic," said Mal uncertainly as we left the bathrooms for the mess hall and breakfast.

"Oh, boy. I hope so."

Parents' Day is quite an affair. People begin arriving around ten. Lunch is at noon, followed by the program, and then ... camp is over and we leave Moose Land.

My parents showed up just before ten-thirty. And they brought Squirt with them! I was so happy. I'd been sure they'd leave our baby brother in Connecticut with a sitter. (What sitter? We were all at Camp Moosehead.)

Anyway, Squirt cooed and gurgled happily when he saw us. He talked his pretend talk. He hardly knows any words, so when he wants to feel grown-up, he babbles to us. "Moy blur-gum star flit?" he said as soon as Becca and I had covered him with kisses. Then Mama and Daddy and Becca and I hugged and hugged.

Becca and I couldn't wait to show our parents around camp, so when Squirt was settled safely in Daddy's backpack, we set off. Becca and I kept calling out things like, "There's the lake! That's where I water-skied!" (That was me.)

"There's the field!" exclaimed Becca. "Charlotte was playing with an archery set there and thought she shot someone but she hadn't."

You'd think that on Parents' Day, we could have had a decent meal, but Old Meanie served those hideous vegetable burgers again. I bet they were left over from Wednesday night. Daddy ate three of them, though. He'll eat anything. Luckily, dessert was ice-cream sundaes.

We were finishing our sundaes when Old Meanie's voice came over the loudspeaker. "Will all campers, CITs, and counselors please assemble at the amphitheater now?" she said. "And will all family members please be seated in the theater by two o'clock?"

"Well," I said to Becca, "this is it. Are you ready?"

She nodded nervously. "Even with my stage fright. I want to dance well for Mama and Daddy, just like you always do."

"Then let's find Mallory and Char and get going."

The amphitheater was a madhouse, but the counselors were good at helping us to organize quickly. Before Mal and I knew it, the time was two o'clock and the program was beginning. The first number was a medley of songs by the campers in 10-A and 10-B. They sang beautifully, didn't make one mistake, and got lots of applause.

Next the six-year-olds put on a short skit.

Then the nine-year-olds performed a scene from the musical *Annie*.

After that — it was our turn.

The girls playing the kids in the neighborhood were the first on stage. They skipped into the amphitheater, twirled around once (somebody fell), then linked arms and began a dancing game. At this point Becca and Char, holding hands, walked on stage. The dancing stopped, the play began. When my sister and Charlotte introduced themselves, I noticed a few raised eyebrows in the audience (including my parents'), but the play went on. Char was trembling and forgot half her lines. At one point, Becca tripped over her. But the crucial part of the play went fine. To demonstrate that the twins finally trusted their new friend, they had to fall backward into her arms, not being caught until they'd just about hit the floor. (This is an extremely difficult thing to do, even with your best friend. Try it sometime. Char fell in every rehearsal because she didn't trust her "catcher" enough and would try to stand up at the last second.) But in the play, she was perfect. So was my sister.

Anyway, when our number was over we actually got a standing ovation.

I guessed we'd made our point. But I wasn't sure until later when Mal and I were back in our cabin, packing the last of our things. All us campers, our CITs, and Autumn, our counselor, were there, but we were totally silent until Autumn said, "Great play, girls. You two did a terrific job with the younger kids."

That broke the ice. I give Mary Oppenheimer a lot of credit for being the first one to say, "Jessi? Mallory? I'm sorry I was mean to you." Because then the other Mary said, "Me, too. Honest." And Mandi said, "If you guys like horse stories, try reading *Impossible Charlie*, by Barbara Morgenroth. It's hysterical."

But Maureen didn't say a word. I guess some people never learn.

It was time to go. Mal and I were packed. Parents and campers were lugging suitcases and boxes and art projects from the cabins to their cars. Mama and Daddy helped with Becca's and my things while I took care of Squirt.

The Pikes had driven to camp in two station wagons. (With eight kids, they always need those two cars.) And it took them forever to pack up Vanessa, Margo, and Mal, on this side of the lake, and Nicky and the triplets on the other side of the lake. By the way, the reunion of Claire and her sisters was really something. They were excited and on their best behavior. But —

"This'll never last," Mal whispered to me. "We'll be fighting before we've even left the parking lot, and then Margo will puke in our Barf Bucket."

I giggled.

I watched Charlotte climb into a car with her mom and dad. I saw Kristy watching her, too.

"I can't believe she stayed for the two weeks," I said to Kristy, shifting Squirt to my other hip.

"Me neither. But you know what she told me last night? She said, 'I made it, Kristy. I didn't know if I could do it, and I did it.' I think that's what Char's camp experience was about. She wanted to prove to herself that she could stay away from home for two weeks, that she was grown-up enough for that. She didn't do it easily, but she did it."

One after another we were leaving. Dawn and Mary Anne got into a car with Mrs. Schafer and Mr. Spier, who had driven to Camp Moosehead together. (Dawn and Mary Anne looked smug and happy about this arrangement.)

Kristy and Karen got into a station wagon loaded with people — Kristy's mom and grandmother, Watson, Andrew, and Emily Michelle — before driving around the lake to pick up David Michael.

And Claudia was picked up by her parents. She'd wanted Mimi to come, but Mimi wasn't feeling well and had stayed at home with Janine taking care of her.

Last but not least, just before my family drove off, I saw Stacey climbing into her parents' car so I rolled down my window and yelled to her, "I'll mail you the diary on Monday!"

And she shouted back, "Okay. Thanks. . . . Have fun and be careful!"

Everyone in her car laughed.

Camp Moosehead was over.

EPILOGUE

Dear Stacey,
   Hello from beautiful stoneybrook!
I'm glad to be back and not glad to
be back. What I mean is, I can't water-
ski here, but it sure is nice to be home
and to see andrew and Emily and
my brothers and everyone. It's
especially nice to be myself again!
   Big Krushers game against the
Bashers coming up. keep your
fingers crossed!

                    Love, Kristy

Dear Stace,
   Hi I'm glad to be back but I'm worryed
abuot Mimi. I dont thinck she feels to
good. Wasn't camp fun, thought? I had a
good time. You will never guess waht. As a
surprize my campers got Will's addres for
me. I don't no how they got it but Vanessa
Pike gave it to me after we were all bake in
Stoneybrooke. Should I writ him a leter?
                         Love,
                              Claud
P.S. Today is the thrid day in a row I've
   worn something with no moose on it.

Dear Stacey,
    How is your poison ivy? I am fine. I am back
at home. I am glad to be here. I can't believe I
hardly ever saw you at camp. Mommy and Daddy
are very proud of me for staying there. They said
i can go to Camp Moosehead next summer
if I want to, but if I don't want to it's all right
and I don't have to.
    I really, really, really, really miss you.
            Love, Charlotte Johanssen

Dear Stacey,
        Merry Christmas!
            Love, Nonie

Thanksh, Nonie, I thought.

Boy, camp sure had generated a lot of mail. Since I love mail, this is fine. One piece of mail I got was from Logan. The envelope contained his diary entries. I stuck them into the diary us girls had been passing around on our side of Lake Whatever.

I *love* having the diary. It's the perfect record of our experiences (good and bad) at Camp Moosehead. In fact, it's a really good book, so I decided to write a few pages at the end to wind things up, and to put in some photographs to illustrate it. Most of us had taken cameras with us to camp, and as we got our film developed, we swapped pictures.

This is how I finished the book:

I, Stacey McGill, am recovered, except from my diabetes, of course. My poison ivy is gone. I hope to heaven that I never get poison ivy again. If I go back to Camp Moosehead, I'll know where not to sit. Nonie and I ended up friends and send each other Christmas cards all the time. Merry Chrishmash, Nonie!

I might as well finish Claudia's story with, "Claudia and Will, sitting in a tree, K-I-S-S-I-N-G!" They haven't actually seen each other since the night of the dance, but Claud *did* decide to write to Will, and he wrote back, so she wrote back, then he wrote back, etc. They didn't have to end their relationship after all.

Kristy is glad to be home and sometimes puts on mascara. Then she puts on her baseball cap and goes out to coach the Krushers. The mascara is in case she runs into Bart coaching the Bashers.

Mary Anne wound up pretty friendly with the other CITs. They write letters sometimes, but Mary Anne says she bets it won't last *too* long. She has also firmly, definitely, positively, certainly, absolutely decided never, ever to have her ears pierced because she cannot forget the sight of that needle coming toward her. She says it appears to her in nightmares, but I think she's kidding.

Dawn, our nature girl, hasn't gotten over her experience in the woods. It scared her, but she's pleased with herself for having gotten through it. She's thinking of signing up for Outward Bound next year. That's where they give you all this survival training, then send you out in the wilderness to be on your own for three days, with nothing but a few matches or something like that. Dawn and Heather write long letters to each other. Heather will not be going back to camp.

Mal and Jessi are still best, best friends.

They'd already read *Impossible Charlie*, by Barbara Morgenroth, but they read it again, because they knew it had taken Mandi courage to tell them about it. Then they wrote to her, saying they'd enjoyed the story. And Mandi wrote back!

So I guess all's well that ends well. I know that's a corny way to finish a book, but Mallory is the writer among us, not me, and this is the best I can do.

The End
by Anastasia Elizabeth McGill
(otherwise known as Stacey)

About the Author

Ann M. Martin's The Baby-sitters Club has sold over 190 million copies and inspired a generation of young readers. Her novels include the Newbery Honor Book *A Corner of the Universe*, *A Dog's Life*, and the Main Street series. She lives in upstate New York.

Keep reading for a sneak peek at the next
Baby-sitters Club Super Special!

Baby-sitters' Winter Vacation

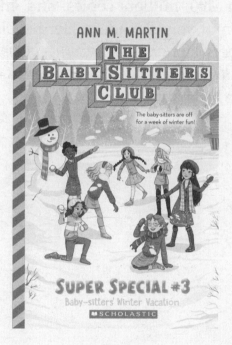

After walking for what seemed like miles, Mrs. George and the teachers began directing large groups of us into various dorms. Each room was so big it could sleep fifty-six people — two rows of fourteen bunk beds each.

"Bunk beds," moaned Stacey. "I'd forgotten. Just like at Camp Moosehead."

"No, *not* just like at Camp Moosehead," I replied. "At camp we didn't have dressers or a rug on the floor or mirrors on the wall."

"Or adjoining bathrooms," added Kristy.

"How am I ever going to find my way around?" wailed Mal as the BSC members, still in a group, continued to follow Mrs. George down the hall.

"We'll have to leave a trail of bread crumbs," said Jessi.

I glanced at Mary Anne and grinned. Then I said, "No, you won't. Really. Last year was my first year here and I thought the same th —"

"Okay, the remaining sixth-grade girls, into this room," called Mr. Bailey, an English teacher.

"They're grouping us by *grades!*" exclaimed Mal in dismay.

We'd been so busy talking we hadn't noticed.

"Did they break us up by grade last year?" I asked Mary Anne.

"I don't remember. I guess so. Anyway, it didn't matter because the BSC members were all in the same grade," she replied.

We said a sad good-bye to Jessi and Mal (I really thought Mal was going to cry), then the last hundred or so of us continued down the hall. We stopped to separate the seventh-grade boys from the eighth-grade girls when we reached the boys' dorm, and then us girls were shown into a final room. Our school filled seven dorms altogether.

Mary Anne, Stacey, Claud, Kristy, and I entered our room.

"Hello, room," said Kristy, who was getting punchy.

"Our home for the next five days," I added.

It really was a very nice room, except for the bunks. But even the bunk beds were a lot nicer than the ones at camp, which looked like someone had tossed a bunch of trees into the cabins and carved the beds out of them right there.

A soft tan carpet covered the floor, and next to each set of bunks was a dresser. Over the dresser was a mirror, and —

"There're the bathrooms!" announced Kristy, pointing to a door at one end of the room.

A few girls dropped their bags and made a dash for the bathrooms. The rest of us scrambled to claim bunk beds. Mary Anne and I got one. (My mom is going out with Mary Anne's dad, and we figured that being bunkies would be good practice in case we ever wound up as stepsisters.) Next to us were Stacey and Claud. Poor Kristy was left without a bunkie and looked sort of sorry for herself.

Then she began to wonder if she would even need a bunkie. "Maybe there are only fifty-four or fifty-five of us," she said excitedly. "I could have a whole bunk to myself. I could sleep on the top tonight, the bottom tomorrow night, the top the third night, the —"

"I don't have a bunkie, Kristy," said a voice from behind us.

Kristy turned around. There was Ashley Wyeth, this spacey, artsy friend of Claudia's. She doesn't have too many good friends besides Claud.

"You don't?" said Kristy. She wanted to be polite, but she couldn't help looking crestfallen.

None of us was sure what to do until Claudia said tactfully, "Hey, why don't Stacey and I move down one bunk, and then Kristy, you and Ashley can be right between Dawn and Mary Anne, and Stacey and me."

"Okay." Kristy managed not to sound *too* reluctant. Then, brightening, she added, "Hey, Ashley, can I have the top bunk?"

Ashley shrugged. "Sure."

Kristy didn't have to worry. Ashley would be a pushover to bunk with. Besides, how could Kristy lose, surrounded by all her friends?

"Come on, you guys, let's unpack," said Stacey. "Then we can go exploring. We don't have to be anywhere until six-thirty, when they serve dinner."

"Go exploring?" I repeated. "We already know where everything is."

"Yeah, but Mal and Jessi don't. And they looked sort of, oh, terrified when we left them. I thought we could give them a tour."

I smiled at Stacey. "Good idea."

So the five of us unpacked quickly. Then we got ready to find the sixth-grade girls' dorm. Claud asked Ashley if she wanted to come with us, but Ashley was sprawled on the floor, sketching. She barely heard the question. We found our way to Mal and Jessi's room and were greeted by cries of, "You found us!" and, "We knew you'd come back!"

I couldn't help laughing. "You guys are supposed to be having *fun*," I pointed out.

"How can we have fun when we don't even know where we are?" asked Mal.

"Look, I'll give you a hint," said Mary Anne. "Every floor is the same, except for the main floor, so you can quit worrying about floors two through four. They're all rooms or dorms. Just learn the way from your dorm to the first floor, okay?"

"Let's go all the way upstairs," said Claud as

the seven of us walked into the hallway. "Then we'll work our way down and prove to them that the second, third, and fourth floors are all the same."

We decided that was a good idea, and took the elevator to the fourth floor.

"See?" I said when the doors opened. "This is just like our floor, the second floor."

"By the way, there's the fourth-floor, D-wing candy machine," added Claud.

We rode to the third floor. "There's the third-floor, D-wing candy machine," said Claud.

We rode to the second floor. "There's *our* candy machine," said Claud.

We rode to the first floor. "There's the dining hall," said Claud as we got off the elevator.

"Home of Claudia's favorite salad bar," I added.

Claud scrunched up her nose and made a horrible face.

"Anyway," said Kristy to Jessi and Mal, "now you know how to get from your dorm to the dining hall."

"Do we have to ride up and look at all the candy machines each time?" asked Jessi, and the rest of us laughed.

"Now we'll show you the really fun stuff," I said. "Follow this hallway in this direction and you come to . . . the common room. This is the main room of the lodge. The check-in desk is here, but it's also a gathering area."

"Look at the fireplace!" said Jessi. "It's so big."

"This is a beautiful room," added Mal.

She was right. The common room was a long, lofty room with beams in the ceiling. It was built of brick and wood. Tables and chairs were grouped for playing board games or cards. There were big easy chairs for reading in. Under our feet was a woolly carpet. Kids and teachers were already drifting down from the dorms. Some of the other guests were finding seats near the fire.

It was just when Jessi was suggesting that we continue the tour that the front door to the lodge burst open, blowing snow onto the carpet, and two nearly frozen people, a man and a woman, staggered inside. The man immediately collapsed on the ground.

"Oh, my lord!" cried Claudia.

A whole bunch of hotel workers rushed to help the people. Someone slammed the door shut. Everyone was asking questions. Finally the woman said, "You've got to help us. Please. We had an accident about two miles down the road. Our bus overturned. We —"

"Bus?" said Mrs. George, making her way

through the crowd. "You're not from Conway Cove Elementary School, are you?"

"Yes! We are!" said the woman. "You must be Mrs. George." (Mrs. George nodded.) "Anyway, I think all the children are okay," the woman went on, "but my arm is fractured — at least, I'm pretty sure it is — and Jim —"

"Jim is going to be fine," spoke up the man on the floor. "I just needed to warm up." He raised his head a little. Then, tentatively, he pulled himself into a sitting position. "See? I'm okay. But we have to get some help back to the kids. They're alone with the bus driver, and he's not in very good shape. He'll need an ambulance. His leg is broken — badly."

"How did you get here?" asked Mrs. George.

"We walked," said the man.

"For two miles? In this weather?" Mrs. George was amazed. And everyone looked outside at the storm, which was growing worse by the second. Then Mrs. George said, "We'll call the police and the rescue squad right away."

Mary Anne and I looked at each other, stunned.

Want more baby-sitting?

And many more!

Don't miss any of the books in the Baby-sitters Club series by Ann M. Martin—available as ebooks

DON'T MISS
THE BABY-SITTERS CLUB
GRAPHIC NOVELS!

graphix

AN IMPRINT OF

SCHOLASTIC

scholastic.com/graphix

BSC

Don't miss any of the books in the Baby-sitters Little Sister series by Ann M. Martin—available as ebooks